Also by Carl Dane:
Hawke and Carmody Western Novels
Valley of the Lesser Evil
Canyon of the Long Shadows

Rapid Fire Reads (short books)
Delta of the Dying Souls

ISBN: 978-1-9997600-9-0

CANYON

OF THE LONG

SHADOWS

A HAWKE & CARMODY WESTERN NOVEL

CARL DANE

RAGING BULL PUBLISHING

Dedication

To Cathy, Mark, and Carl.
With love.

Chapter 1

When I told Judge Percival Weed that I had evidence he'd taken a bribe, he told me he was holding me in contempt and would put me in jail.

I told Judge Weed that as I was the marshal and it was *my* jail, I would be damned if I'd check myself in.

He tilted his head back and told me in the squeaky, clipped tone favored by snippy little fussbudgets everywhere that we had *something of a dilemma, now don't we?*

I assured him that we had nothing of the kind and grabbed a handful of his shirt, necktie and whatever else he was wearing underneath that robe and pulled him over the top of the bar where he'd set up court.

In addition to a robe, the pretentious little peckerwood had actually brought a *gavel* with him when setting up an impromptu court in the Silver Spoon, a combination bar and bordello run by my sometime girlfriend, Elmira Adler. Bar-room courts are not unusual in the various ass ends of central Texas – they are, in fact, the norm, as most small towns didn't have courthouses – but robes and gavels were a bit much, and I particularly objected to the gavel when he hit me on the shoulder with it.

It stung, so I took it away and yanked him up to his full height of maybe five and a half feet and lifted him off the ground by half an inch or so. I'm not a particularly big man, a little over six feet and on the lean side, but I'd spent a decade as a prize-fighter. In that line of work you learn about leverage and how to use your legs to lift an opponent off-balance.

You also learn about how effective a weapon intimidation can be.

"Judge Weed," I said, "assuming that you are a real judge of some yet-to-be determined species, I have a question on which I would welcome a ruling."

He said nothing. I'm not sure he could. He was only able to gurgle a little – I was lifting him by a big handful of cloth in my right hand and was cutting off most of his air – and he did a panicky little toe-dance.

"Do you see this gavel?" I held it with my left hand about two inches in front of his face and his eyes crossed as he looked at it. "Do you think it will hurt more going in or when the doctor pulls it out?"

With that he began to sob and then he marched dutifully to his cell – and thus began my troubles with the entire judiciary of Texas, several of its politicians, a substantial portion of the state's criminal class, and the considerable overlap among those groups.

Chapter 2

Let me back up a little.

My name is Josiah Hawke and I'm the marshal in Shadow Valley, a dismal little hamlet that I must admit is not without its charms, including Elmira, but I'll get to her in a minute. I was brought here about a year ago to find the killer of the former marshal, Billy Gannon.

Gannon was my captain in the war. We were part of a Union detachment that specialized in what you might categorize as "special tactics" or "dirty tricks," your point of view depending on whether you were doing them or having them done to you. After the regiment was mustered out in June of 1865, I returned to my life as a professor at a small Illinois college, and Billy turned to lawing.

My educational career ended a month later when a pug with a traveling carnival goaded me into fighting him. I handled him pretty easily – I would imagine he regarded my sneak right hand, which I could land pretty much at will, as a dirty trick. He tried to gouge out my eye in retaliation.

I took exception to that and beat him to death and left town one step ahead of the law. As do a lot of men technically categorized as outlaws, I found occasional work enforcing the law (the skill set is mostly interchangeable) and also put together a pretty good record as an itinerant bareknuckle prize-fighter.

I had lost contact with Billy for ten years after the war and was reunited with his corpse after Elmira contacted me. He'd told her to wire me if anything happened to him. Which it did. He caught four bullets to the head.

It would take a very tough man to kill Billy Gannon.

I found the man who did it, and he *was* tough, but I killed him anyway.

His name was Purcell. He was a gunfighter, a pro as quick as a rattler and just as mean. He'd been nebulously connected to a network of shadowy creatures who tried to drive Elmira out of business so they could lay claim to the land in back of her place. The property was essentially a worthless expanse of brush, until whatever spider lay in the midst of the plot learned of the plans for a shiny new railroad right through the acreage.

As I heaved the little man who had slithered into town and announced himself as a "special territorial magistrate" into my modest little iron-bar hotel, I wondered if I'd just sent the first faint vibration radiating toward the center of that web.

Chapter 3

Tom Carmody, my deputy, sat on the bench in front of the office and whittled.

I didn't know anyone outside of a rube character in a play or dime novel who actually sits for hours and whittles, but Carmody does. He's from the hills of Eastern Tennessee and even though he now favors bowlers and vested suits he somehow makes them look like straw hats and overalls.

He chews tobacco as well as whittles and leaves a hell of a mess everywhere, but he keeps saving my life, so I have no choice but to keep him around.

"Shit, it's hot in there," Carmody said. It came out, *sheee-it, it's hot in thar.* "But the little fucker won't take off his robe."

"Really."

"Yup. That's 'cause when you gave him the stink-eye he pissed himself. Don't want it to show. I noticed the puddle in the cell."

I sat down next to Carmody. There wasn't a lot of room, as he's about six-five and tends to sit splay-legged.

He rubbed his wiry black beard, as is his wont when he has something on his mind. When he wants to make an intelligent point – which he is extraordinarily capable of doing, though not on a regular schedule – he generally thinks before he speaks. When he wants to get under my skin, he just blurts like a Gatling gun.

"It occurs to me," he said, "that we might not find an easy way out of this. You just threw a judge in jail and wasn't too hospitable doing it."

"First off, I'm not entirely sure he's a real judge. He waltzed in here claiming he's a 'territorial magistrate.' That may very well be true. The state hands out titles like Easter candy, mostly to the donor class or people connected to them. Whether being a 'territorial magistrate' equates to being a real judge I'm not sure. I've never heard of a 'territorial magistrate.' But there are plenty of freelance judges – and marshals, for that matter – of what you might call dubious provenance."

Carmody sliced off another sliver of wood and held the stick up for inspection, as though he were contemplating his next chisel cut in a marble statue.

"Kinda like us," he said.

"True enough."

Carmody and I had been duly appointed by the town council – at least we had a contract and got paid – but in actuality no one in town is quite sure who's on the council or how they got elected or even how many members are supposed to constitute it. Elmira sort of inherited her seat from her late husband. There's a sour-faced druggist named

Miller who vaguely indicated that he regards himself as a councilman. And there are other councilmen who meet with Elmira in secret but won't reveal their identity because they're afraid of getting murdered by the same people who tried to kill me and Carmody.

Elmira felt badly about keeping their names secret from me, but I assured her that if she gave her word to them she'd get no complaint from me for keeping it.

If our political system in Shadow Valley seems haphazard, it is. But it's not atypical in a town made up largely of drifters and people allergic by nature to laws and lawmakers.

There is only one person in town that had any political ambition, and his name is Jefferson Gillis. He comes and goes but returned in a big way a week ago. He's a self-styled political reformer who has a big mouth and a grand opinion of himself and probably emerged from the birth canal with an ulterior motive.

I took an immediate dislike to him when I first met him last week, and determined that he very well might wind up as a guest in my little cell. I'd never had two people in there. Now, it would be cramped as well as damp.

Gillis was apparently going to force the decision because he was walking down the street with seven men wearing sidearms.

Chapter 4

Gillis brought up the rear, marching to his own monologue as he intoned his unending list of grievances. He was perpetually aggrieved, as far as I could determine, and rarely stopped talking. The men accompanying him would occasionally grunt a *yeah* or a *that's right,* but their hearts weren't in it. They just wanted to hurt me and get it over with. While I didn't recognize them, I knew their type: hard-eyed, down-on-their-luck drifters who hired themselves out as muscle.

"...and you assaulted a legally-appointed magistrate." He was drifting into earshot.

"You and your cowboys stop right there," I said.

I'm old-school. Though I hear some people use the word "nowadays" to refer to anybody on the trail, when I was a kid, "cowboy" usually implied a rustler or petty criminal. That's how I meant it, and I got a couple of glares from those who picked up my meaning.

They did honor my command to stop, but not before they'd shuffled into a semi-circle around me and Carmody. We'd stepped into the street to greet them.

Gillis, of course, just kept talking.

"And I protest!" He drawled it out, *ahhhhhhh pro-TEST*, in an overly broad cadence. I happened to find out he grew up in New Jersey. He didn't quite have the inflection down, although he did do a very convincing imitation of someone imitating a politician, maybe one from Texas, though the lilt suggested Louisiana or Arkansas.

"I'm guessing your magistrate is some minor government functionary with a fancy title," I said, "and you paid him to come down here to cook up a reason for you to grab Elmira Adler's property."

"You are so typical," Gillis said, "of the jackal pack always at the throat of someone seeking honest and fair representation. You, sir," – it came out *suh* – "are *despicable.*"

I took a moment and just looked at him. People who feed on drama are unnerved when their supply is cut off. Whenever possible I like to keep people off-balance, especially when they are hiding behind a gang of goons who appear to have imminent battery on their minds.

Gillis was tall, carried a few extra pounds, and had a bulbous nose. I pegged him at about 40, although his hair was prematurely gray. He owned property at the edge of town, though he'd not been around for a year. Gillis owned some sort of cattle operation, I'm told, which keeps him in the eastern part of the state most of the time.

Some of the girls at the Spoon told me they remembered Gillis, who had a habit of showing up every couple years or so and causing a commotion, and then disappearing as suddenly as he'd arrived. Gillis was somehow involved in the fringes of politics, in a murky, undefined way. He liked to make deals and speeches, and described himself as an advocate for justice. He also liked to pontificate in public about how the girls in the Spoon's employ were exploited, but in private he enjoyed getting drunk, slapping them around, and when he really got cucumbered, talking like he was from New Jersey.

Oddly, when I asked her, Elmira would only say that he meant well.

"Don't you have anything to say?" Gillis asked, impatient. I'd thrown a wrench into his machinery. In Gillis's world, when you publicly condemned a man he was supposed to get huffy and sputter a defense. He was itchy waiting for the echo that never came. The laws of his universe were malfunctioning, and he didn't like it at all.

So I stared at him a little longer while I tried to figure out what the game was.

At present, the man's motivation eluded me, but Shadow Valley was a place of half-truths and unspoken secrets. I suppose every place is like that, more or less.

All I knew was that he'd ridden into town three days ago and claimed that according to town bylaws, the Silver Spoon was "unlawful" – his words – because the rules only allowed one drinking establishment.

He further claimed that the present government of the town was "unlawful" – again, that word, which sounds like "illegal" but it's not, hence a good way to rouse some indignation without having to be too specific – because we could not produce records of the vote.

Well, he had a point. Shadow Valley, and probably hundreds of sorry little hamlets like it in this area, are barely more than shantytowns. Over the years, settlers had come and gone, setting up by-laws and ordinances that melted away as quickly as the previous wave of drifters.

Back in the days when I was a teacher, I would expound on the structure of government. It sounded so damn tidy when I read it from the pages of a book. But in the decade or so I've spent alternately enforcing laws and running away from them, I've seen that in most parts of the West the laws are conflicting, varying among jurisdictions, muddled as to what jurisdiction actually holds authority, and pretty much like the rules of prizefighting – made up on the spot by the referee, and then pretty much nonexistent once the first punch is thrown.

So in keeping with that spirit, I decided to throw it.

It was a clean straight right hand to the chin of the cowboy nearest to me.

He obligingly fell flat on his back, arms outspread, and I bent over him and took his pistol, handing it over my shoulder to Carmody.

Chapter 5

Gillis didn't seem accustomed to violence. Shocked as he was, he actually couldn't come up with a speech, which was an unexpected treat. He just stuttered a little. So I figured now was a good time to say my piece.

"I asked about those 'bylaws' you keep quoting," I said, "and they were drawn up twenty years ago by people who are no longer in this town and likely no longer on this earth."

"The law...the law..."

"Come on, Gillis. Spit it out."

He made a conscious effort to compose himself and lectured me that the law is the law and stays the law until it's changed.

Carmody spoke up.

"The doctrine of *stare decisis*," he said. "Latin for 'the decision stands.'"

I didn't want to turn away from the six goons who remained vertical, but I couldn't help but shoot him a glance over my shoulder.

"How do you *know* this stuff?

For a guy who'd spent most of his life in the mountains jumping stumps and eating squirrels, Carmody had a stunning range of knowledge. Sometimes I'd play the upright piano in the Spoon and sneak in a modified version of Mozart or Beethoven – Carmody called them "cowpoked up" – and he'd usually be able to summon up the composer and title.

"I ain't no dummy," he said. "Wasn't no fancy professor and military officer like you, but I do some reading when I have a chance."

"And why are you taking his side?"

"I ain't. My point is that there ain't no precedent unless a law's been used by the court, and as we don't have no courts here and the only judge is a phony little pissant who pissed on his robe, Gillis's argument don't hold water any better than the phony judge does."

Gillis's goons were getting restless. They'd been hired to rough up a marshal, not listen to a mountain man lecture them on jurisprudence. Can't say I wouldn't have felt the same way, to tell you the truth.

In any event, I was getting tired of the entire piece of street theater.

"Gillis," I said, "you're orchestrating an attack on a sworn peace officer. That's a felony. It's also stupid. That adds up to felonious stupidity, and I'm a heartbeat away from arresting you for it. And maybe I might throw in bribing a judge. Carmody saw you hand Weed a fistful of money at the delta fork."

"That's *impossible,*" Gillis said.

And then he realized that he'd just made a tacit confession, but he made a quick recovery.

"*Impossible* that a man of Judge Weed's integrity would take a bribe, and equally absurd that I would be involved in something like that."

"Carmody could see you just fine. He's from a long line of mountain ancestors. We're not sure of his family tree, but apparently one of them was a goat because he likes to climb up high and keep an eye on things. Good quality in a deputy. He was on the roof of the bank when Weed rode in on the trail through the delta."

The town's one and only bank had been built at the fork of two rivers, an unlikely place for a bank because it regularly flooded. More improbably, the bank was rebuilt on the same spot after it burned down, a conflagration that was partly my fault. But that's another story for another time.

"I did not bribe that judge – Mr. Weed." Gillis spoke slowly and decisively, wagging his finger in that earnest manner employed by experienced liars.

"He ain't no real judge anyway," Carmody said.

"He *is* a real judge and you are *not* real lawmen," Gillis said. "You were appointed by the madame of a whorehouse who claims that she *inherited* her seat from the husband I suspect she killed anyway."

He was close. Elmira hadn't killed her husband; her daughter did. That, too, is another story.

Gillis liked the sound of his own voice and he was picking up momentum, like a locomotive headed downhill.

He stopped wagging his finger and poked it in the air.

"These men and I have formed a committee to reconstitute the rule of law in this town. You are *not* duly sworn officers and we *demand* that you stand down. Isn't that right, men?"

A gigantically fat fellow with a flowing beard mechanically said, "Yeah." Some kid with buck teeth and red hair and little eyes nodded. And a thin fellow in the back spit and rolled his eyes and spoke up.

"Can we just bust him up now and get this over with, Mr. Gillis?"

I'd suspected from the start that Gillis's plan was to lay a group beating on me. I didn't think they'd risk gunplay because even in a more or less lawless territory, killing a lawman – even one of dubious heritage – could still be trouble. And if they wanted to kill me outright, why not a simple rifle shot from down the street?

Of course, there was always the possibility that I'd shoot *them,* but that's whey they'd swarmed me on the pretense of registering Gillis's protest. And maybe they'd figured that as a peace officer – of doubtful provenance or not – I'd feel constrained by the law, or some moral code, not to capriciously ventilate them. And they had a point.

But the matter was coming to a head. The odds were against us, and the one on the ground had regained consciousness, struggling to a sitting position.

I had no professional or ethical qualms about keeping a downed opponent from getting up and rejoining the effort to dismantle me, however, so I kicked him in the head.

He flattened back out again.

"And Gillis," I said, "I told you that I'd asked about those town bylaws you swear by. They also prohibit carrying a gun within the town limits. I'm not really sure where the town limits are. Nobody seems to know. But seeing as how we're smack in the center of town, I figure they must be in force here."

And with that I used a short left hook to the temple of the next-closest goon. He was out before he fell, and I snatched his revolver from his holster as he crumpled.

The remaining five cowboys closed in.

Gillis stepped back to watch.

Chapter 6

I kept my hands clasped in front of me at waist level. It was a peaceful-looking posture, but it hid the fact that I was tensing with my left hand, trying to slash out from my body, but restraining the movement of my left hand with my right.

When I let go of my left hand, it moved in an explosive arc. You can strike like a cobra by holding and releasing in that manner, and the edge of my hand chopped the guy to my left cleanly across the throat. It took a second to register, and then I saw his eyes go wide with shock and pain. I forced myself to direct my attention elsewhere; the last thing you want to do in my business is stop to admire your work. He would be out of commission for a while and I had other business to attend to – to be precise, to my right and about six feet away.

I turned sideways and snapped out a kick to his knee. The knee is a vulnerable part of the body, what with that little plate of soft tissue that crumples up so conveniently when the edge of a hard boot slices into it. The fellow I'd kicked, the skinny kid who urged Gillis to get on with my beating, had been taking a step forward when I crushed his knee and the timing was perfect. He stepped onto a leg that would no longer bear weight and collapsed face-first, his hat falling off in the process. I kicked him square in the top of the head, the place where a bundle of nerves join together, I've been told.

He jerked a couple of times and went limp, face-down.

There were four of them left and two were trying to get in back of me, but they encountered a formidable barrier in Carmody, who was a wrestler by inclination.

One of Gillis's goons had grabbed Carmody from the rear and cinched his arms around his waist. Carmody snapped both their bodies backward, which was probably the very last thing the guy who'd grabbed him from behind expected. Instead of falling flat on his back, at the very last moment Carmody arched upward, driving the attacker's head and neck into the hard dirt of the road.

Carmody was up in a second, agile as a cat, and it occurred to me that it was genuinely awe-inspiring to see a man that large move so quickly.

The guy he'd pole-driven head-first into the dirt, I surmised, probably would not get up anytime soon.

Suddenly the odds were three to two, not counting Gillis, who had gone pale and was backing away, unsure of whether to stay or run.

The most formidable remaining goon, very fat but thick-necked and broad-shouldered, with a beard and long hair, surveyed the situation. He apparently decided that the odds were still with him, and he put his head down and charged me.

There's only one foolproof response to that, and it was taught to me by a fighter who'd spent some time in Siam, where they fight with knees and elbows as well as feet and fists.

I grabbed two convenient handfuls of his hair and beard – it wasn't clear where one boundary left off other the other started – and jerked his head down. At the same time, I brought my knee up to his face. If you practice, and I had, you can put your whole body into the movement and generate enormous power.

The wick behind his eyes flickered out instantly, but his momentum carried him forward. I was off-balance and on one foot and he shoved me backward, falling on top of me. He was doughy of build and heavy as a horse, and I was pinned under a mass of flesh that oozed and flowed as I pushed on it, as though his unconscious body was keeping up the fight on its own. I couldn't get any leverage.

Now there were two of them left, other than Gillis, who had backed away some more and looked as though he wanted to cry.

The two looked at Carmody and did not like what they saw. He has one of those powerful backwoods builds, long and rangy with thick wrists, ropey veins, and huge hands.

And that's when the one with the buck teeth began reaching for his gun. He moved hesitantly, like somebody does looking while over their shoulder when they really don't want to see what's behind them.

I was afraid a gun would come out. As much as I wouldn't have minded plugging him, gunfire would add a new and unwelcome dimension to the friendly little beating they had planned to lay on us, both a legal dimension and an escalation of the type of revenge each party would seek after the smoke had cleared and the bodies were buried.

Carmody was just disposing of the other conscious attacker – holding him by the collar and alternatively backhanding and forehanding him into insensibility – and if Bucktooth went for his weapon, Carmody would have no choice but to drill him.

I wanted to do something but was still pinned under an elephant-full of flesh that flowed with a mind of its own. I couldn't buck him off and was losing my breath from trying. My feet were free, but I was too far away to kick with any effect. I was, however, able to hook my heel in back of Bucktooth's and press my other heel into the front of his knee. That pushed him straight back and he fell flat.

Carmody finished off his opponent with a smart backhand and reached down, seizing Bucktooth's gun hand.

"Do you really want to travel down this road?"

Bucktooth stiffened and he had something of a spasm as he tried to pull his weapon. His eyes grew wider as the slow realization overtook him:

Carmody's grip was like something set by a stone-mason.

Carmody backhanded him into unconsciousness.

As strong as he was, Carmody had to heave the elephant three times to unearth me from blubbery captivity. As we pried the monster off me, he made strange sputtering noises with this lips.

Now we had a dilemma. First, it's not easy to carry seven extra revolvers. Carmody and I filled up our pockets and our waistbands and tucked a couple inside our shirts, but we clanked when we walked. I had a fleeting worry that we might set one off by accident if we dropped it.

Second, we had seven thugs in various states of incapacitation who were gradually rousing themselves. At most, we could squeeze one extra person into my cell, and the guy with the beard would probably need his own individual barn. We could chain them to trees or something – it wouldn't be the first time we'd employed that particular manner of detention – but doing so would entail a host of other inconveniences. We decided to keep their guns and let them walk away as soon as they were willing and able, assuming they would have the sense to stay peaceful and avoid another beating.

Finally, there was the matter of Gillis, who was frozen in terror and made no effort to run. Locking him up would be trouble because he was, as far as I could determine, well-connected; putting him behind bars would be his ticket to political martyrdom, which I sensed he would enjoy.

Still, he had orchestrated an attack on a marshal and deputy and that's worth a couple days of penance, I concluded.

Carmody agreed, and we marched him to the cell, stopping only to pick up the occasional revolver that dropped out of our pockets and waistbands on our way. I tensed up every time one fell.

Carmody steered Gillis into the cell, where he would share about thirty square feet with Judge Percival Weed.

"Mind your step," Carmody said, leading Gillis in. "Floor's a might damp and slippery."

Chapter 7

As was usual, I woke long before Elmira and watched her sleep until it came time for me to forcibly pry her into consciousness.

She was a beautiful woman. No kid, to be sure, but neither am I. Her hair was like spun precious metal, part gold, part silver, and a trace of platinum. Her eyes were big and round, blue as a mountain lake, and childlike in the sense that they appeared to be perpetually delighted, seeing everything anew for the first time.

I rather doubted there was one facet of human degradation she had not witnessed by now, and I was prepared to be enraptured by the incongrous innocence of her eyes as soon as she managed to open them.

Elmira had been raised by Apaches who had killed part of her family but adopted the rest. Such selective slaughter and domesticity within one group of captives certainly didn't make sense to my way of thinking, but I've learned that reasoning is a process of a culture and things don't necessary conform to any universal laws of logic because there aren't any.

Elmira's daughter, Cassie, was half-Apache. Her father was killed by Comanches a year or so before Elmira ran away and returned to white life, first as a prostitute – as she tells it, the only option available to a woman who had been a long-term guest of the Apaches – and later as a partner in the Silver Spoon with her late husband. Cassie had lived with Elmira until a year ago. Cassie had killed her stepfather, Bannister Adler, Elmira's husband, because he'd repeatedly raped her, something I found out in the process of investigating the murder of Marshal Billy Gannon. Cassie then went to live with an Apache chief named Taza, which I knew would be rough road but one suited for her; she was a tough girl with many demons that overtook her mind when she had too much time to think about them.

As I say, there is little in this world that Elmira's eyes haven't seen.

"You're awake," she said, noticing that I was watching her.

I didn't think that needed confirmation, so I let it pass.

"I've been thinking about Jefferson Gillis," she said.

"Kind of a strange thought to begin the morning with. But go ahead."

"Maybe it's not fair that you put him in jail."

I sat upright.

"Why in hell not? He tried to have me and Carmody beaten up, and from the looks of it, maybe beaten to death."

"Well, maybe that was at least partly your fault. He has a right to be a political activist. Things just got out of hand."

"Elmira, he's *active* in trying to *put you out of business.*"

"I don't think that's the reason. At least you can hear him out and not toss him behind bars. He *does* have good ideas. He was in the Spoon early yesterday and told the girls he favors women getting the right to vote. Did you know that just about five years ago Texas was considering putting the women's vote in the state constitution? But it was killed in a committee or something, whatever that means. He said if *he* were there he would have made sure it went through."

I leaned back on an elbow and contemplated the coming excursion though some dangerous territory.

"First," I said, keeping my tone neutral, "he wasn't there, and never will be there, if 'there' means being at the capital making laws. He's a con man and an opportunist and has nothing to do with government other than currently enjoying the municipal hospitality of the Shadow Valley jail."

"But his *ideas* are good. He cares."

"Elmira, he slaps your girls around when he gets drunk. He's nibbling around the edge of some crooked deal to seize your land. But you say he *cares?*"

She yanked the covers up to her neck and spun away from me, taking all the covers with her.

"You're just jealous."

I was, but not in the way she suspected.

I was and remain truly envious about how some people lie and cheat and still get people to like them.

Or vote for them.

Wish I knew how to do that.

So I turned in the other direction and went back to sleep, even though I was cold.

Chapter 8

Later in the morning I sent a telegram to State Senator Thaddeus Munro, my one and only important friend in politics. He'd been a major in my unit, an Academy man with a classical understanding of tactics and strategy but an open mind toward what you might call nontraditional warfare.

Munro liked straight talk, which seems to me to be at odds with his present career, but despite his bluntness he is not without his charms and unique graces.

I received a reply late in the afternoon.

TO HAWKE, MARSHAL

YOU HAVE REALLY STEPPED IN SHIT STOP WEED REALLY IS SORT OF A JUDGE AND POLITICALLY CONNECTED STOP BUT IF YOU AGREE TO DO BIG FAVOR FOR SUPREME COURT JUDGE YOU CAN HANG THE LITTLE FUCKER FOR ALL WE CARE STOP HARBOLD WILL RIDE TO YOUR PITIFUL LITTLE TOWN TOMORROW WITH DETAILS

MUNRO

Chapter 9

Munro didn't say when Tom Harbold would arrive, but I knew that Austin was at least a two-hour ride, and so he'd probably be there by late morning.

When I stopped in at the Spoon after my morning rounds, Elmira was already packing lunch for the prisoners.

She had a habit of picking up strays, a trait I ordinarily admired. Down-and-outers could always put the touch on her for a free meal, and if the doctor wasn't around she'd take it upon herself to patch up whomever I'd whacked over the head that day. She'd tended in a motherly way to Bucktooth, the last of the Gillis gang to remain horizontal, yesterday in the bar. All the rest of Gillis's thugs had recovered the ability to walk upright and melted away to whatever place lowlifes go to brood and plot revenge, but we had to pick up and carry Bucktooth because he was blocking traffic and the stage couldn't get through.

Carmody's backhand had seriously rearranged the kid's brainpan and opened up a deep gash on his cheekbone. Bucktooth kept issuing some sort of mewling plaint as he sat on a barstool and

Elmira swabbed turpentine on the cut. It sounded like *waba-waba-waba-something,* but I couldn't make it out and didn't care.

Elmira clucked her tongue throughout the process and fixed me with a look of cold reproach.

The same look I was getting as I sat and watched her stuff bread into a wicker basket.

"Look," I said, "I don't understand why you're mad at *me.* Those goons were hired muscle who were going to put our lights out. And it was Carmody who scrambled that hayseed's eggs, not me."

She rolled her eyes and blew out through pursed lips and gave me that look that implied I will never understand her, which is completely correct.

"It's not that," she said. "Not completely. I can't make judgments because I didn't see it. Maybe they were out to hurt you, like you *claim,* or maybe, like Mr. Gillis says, they were lawfully trying to take a stand."

"Shit," I said. "He's got you brainwashed to the point where you're even talking like him. You saw that bunch prying themselves off the road. Did any of them look like Henry David Thoreau?"

She didn't follow.

"Why? Who's that? Is he wanted for something?"

I went from walking carefully to tiptoeing through the conversation. Elmira is a sharp businesswoman, but is as deaf to sarcasm as she is to musical pitch. She also displays a dogged persistence in taking things literally. Once, after a few too many whiskeys we got into a heated disagreement about somebody I believed had duped her and I asked her if she knew the word "gullible" was not in the dictionary.

We don't have a schoolhouse in Shadow Valley, much less any dictionaries, but a couple months later she was on a trip to Austin, found herself near a library, and checked.

When she returned, she matter-of-factly informed me I was *wrong.* I let it pass.

The moral is that I have to be careful of what I say.

"Thoreau was a guy who didn't believe much in government," I said. "And he didn't believe you had to obey the law if the law was wrong. He wouldn't pay taxes he thought were going to unjust causes. Wrote a book about it – 'Civil Disobedience.'"

"Sounds sensible."

"I agree, though there have to be limits and common sense. If Mr. Thoreau were about to have his brains beat in by a gang of hired thugs, I'm sure he'd pony up his tax money to pay a marshal. There are people like him who sit in a cabin and write, and there are people like me who keep squatters from stealing his cabin. It's all a part of the grand scheme of things."

She nodded and said *uh-huh* and I could see this conversation was going nowhere.

"My point is that there are bad people in the world who pretend to be good people. Gillis is *not* a good person. He's trying to put you out of business, for one thing."

"He never said that," she said, covering the bread with a napkin. "He said that the town bylaws called for the electorate to determine the number of drinking and gambling houses. Right now, it's set at one. But we can obviously *change* that. That's what he said; I don't want to put the Full Moon out of business any more than Eddie wants to put *me* out of business. But maybe two *should* be the limit. If there's too much competition, everybody goes out of business, and then there's no business."

The Full Moon was owned by Eddie Moon, hence the name of the joint. We'd had dealings with Moon, an amiably ruthless sort of fellow who had a quick smile but would put his own mother out of business if she happened to own a competing whorehouse.

He was back East visiting family now, and normally he would be first on my list of suspects who were complicit in the goings-on, but I'd heard him mention the planned trip more than six months ago and I doubted anybody around here hatched plots with that long a gestational period.

"But don't you see?" Elmira continued. "If Mr. Gillis cleans up the town government we can set the limit on bars at two. That's what he promised. That's fair."

She left out discussion of her other product line, but it was understood.

"You know what happens in these types of towns," she said. "Somebody with a lot of money swoops in."

She accentuated the word by sweeping her hand through the air.

"*Swoops* in and sets up a place overnight. It's not hard to do. Steals everybody else's business, milks the town dry, and moves on. What Mr. Gillis wants to do, well, it may not seem like it, but he explained it and he says it's for my own good."

I wondered for a moment whether someday some very smart scientist would invent a machine that could somehow sum up the vast total cosmic damage inflicted under the banner of *he says it's for my own good.*

She put her hands on her hips.

"But he can't do anything locked up in that tiny little cell," she said.

I picked up the basket.

"I'll drop it off. I have to head over to the office anyway. I torture the political prisoners every day at noon."

Elmira tended to take things literally, and for a second I thought she believed I was really going to do it.

For a second, I might have considered it. But only for a second.

Chapter 10

Tom Harbold walked into my office right after I'd given each prisoner a separate outhouse break, listened to their complaints, and deposited Elmira's food basket on the cot for them to fight over.

"The little guy still has his robe on," Harbold said.

"Long story. Let's take a walk."

"Yes, sir."

I held the door for him.

"I'm not a 'sir' any more, Tom. In the grand scheme of things, you probably outrank me now. 'Deputy State Constable.' Pretty impressive."

"It's not a bad job, Lieutenant."

I saw no point in correcting him again.

"And I get this nice uniform, a regular salary, and a cavalry-trained horse."

"And the chance to travel to beautiful little havens like Shadow Valley to straighten out problems involving jailed judges."

"There is that," Harbold said.

We stopped. We'd reached the end of town, no one was in earshot, and the scenery wasn't worth a trip back.

Harbold retrieved some tobacco and rolling papers. He offered me one, but I declined. I'm not opposed to tobacco in principle and indulge on occasion, but it cuts my wind. Harbold rolled it with one hand, making it seem effortless, as he did with most things.

Medium-tall, he was lean and had wavy blonde hair and that air of unflappable poise that made him popular both with commanders and subordinates. He was a tough guy and looked the part: His eyes were blue and cold and his face, while good-looking in the conventional sense, projected unconscious disdain for those less handsome and fashionable.

He was, therefore, catnip to the ladies, and given my current icy relations with Elmira I thought better of inviting him to the Spoon for a drink so as not to be unjustly accused of jealously should she hover around him like a moth.

"Major Munro says you've really stepped in it this time, Sir. The little asshole actually *is* sort of a judge. He was appointed to make rulings in cases involving land disputes and railroad and telegraph lines, things like that. Mind you, he's supposed to sit in an office and fill out forms. Nobody expected him to go freelance and set up court like he did here, apparently with the intent of issuing some rulings on the land rights of your lady friend. Whether he can really do that and hold people in contempt, most notably you, is something that'll have to be kicked up the totem pole. Meanwhile, your ass will be in the wind while it's being decided. And I don't have to tell you it's all about roaches going after crumbs from the railroad project."

"Who appointed Weed?"

"Nobody and everybody," Harbold said. "These commissions and magistrates and territorial rings and the like come out of nowhere and are justified by fine print in laws that are enacted by statues that created commissions that wrote new regulations setting up new bureaucracies, and...well, you get the picture. One big circle with no beginning or end. Guess the government is *us,* though. We create these things and have to live with them. Remember, that whole litany of complaints I just spouted is coming from a well-paid 'deputy constable.' I get a hell of a nice horse, too. Did I mention that?"

I laughed, but he didn't. It wasn't his style, as he was too sophisticated to smile at his own joke. And it made me laugh harder.

He stubbed out his smoke and gave me the look that indicated he was no longer pretending to be serious, but was now seriously being serious.

"Major Munro – *Senator* Munro – says he can make it all go away if you can do something. Not for him, but for a big-time Austin judge who's politically connected up the ass. The major says he'd clear you in a second if he could, but this is out of his control. But the judge can fix it."

Harbold rolled another cigarette. He liked creating suspense.

"And," he said, puffing, closing one eye against the coiling smoke, "in case you're worried, you're not being asked to do anything illegal. The major says it's the right thing to do. Lives are in danger. It's an emergency. It has to be handled fast and handled in secret."

"Why me?"

Harbold shrugged. "For one thing, this judge who needs a favor specifically asked for you. He knows the major and knows the major knows you. You've got quite a reputation, even up in Austin. I read that story in the paper about how you shot the revolver out of that gunfighter's hand."

For the record, someone I once knew who nursed an old grudge ambushed me and I drew wild and got off a panic shot. The round very well could have gone into the ceiling or the floor. Or into my leg, and I sort of wish it had. Instead, it most improbably hit the tip of his gun barrel and tore the weapon out of his grasp.

Harbold knew that no one could shoot a gun out of someone else's hand, at least on purpose. Anyone who knew anything at all about weaponry knew it too. But your average drunken cowboy might not and could think twice about trying to shoot me, so while I like accuracy in journalism, I am not above a little self-serving propaganda if it keeps me from getting ventilated.

"Also," Harbold said, "in addition to the fact that you can do magic tricks, the major knows you've got your tit in a wringer and he can bargain away your judge problem because the person who needs your help is the guy who handles matters involving the judiciary. In other words, he judges the judges."

I nodded, knowing there was more.

"And while I hate to phrase it this way," Harbold said, "he knows you're crazy enough to take on a job knowing it's very likely to get you killed."

I agreed to the assessment of my mental health but said that I still needed to know what the hell was going on before I committed.

Harbold told me. When he finished, I asked him to tell the major I'd handle it.

"Yes, Sir," Harbold said, mounted his gleaming, seventeen-hand-high horse, and saluted.

"And Tom, please don't call me 'sir.'"

"Is that an order, Sir?"

"I can't give you orders."

"Then you can't tell me not to call you 'Sir,' Sir."

He had me on that one.

He rode off.

Chapter 11

Harbold had talked with the only witness who had escaped and relayed the story to me.

It all started when the stage to Austin was halted by a fallen tree blocking the road.

Stagecoach drivers know that ninety-nine times out of a hundred when a tree blocks the trail, it's because the thing fell down because of wind or a lightning strike.

But they're not stupid, and they understand that there's always the one percent of the time when it's an ambush.

Smart drivers usually handle it by stopping the stage far enough away from the impediment that they can turn and head back the way they came if need be. The shotgun rider surveys the area as best as he can and he and the driver, both armed and alert, approach the tree on foot. Sometimes the driver, with some help from the guard and the passengers, is able to move the obstruction. But trees are heavy, and there's no room on a stagecoach to carry timber saws, so sometimes you just have to surrender and find an alternate route.

On this particular stage there were a driver, a guard, and three passengers. The guard, named

Burnell, was too smart for his own good. He told the driver that the best course of action would be to avoid possible trouble and a backache from trying to clear the tree; backtrack a mile or so up the steep hill they had just descended, he advised, and take the trail a little to the south. It was a little rougher but would rejoin the main road well before the post where they'd change to a fresh team of horses.

The driver didn't like the idea of prodding the tired team up the steep incline but liked the idea of trying to move the tree a lot less.

The driver, guard, and passengers relaxed as much as they could in a jolting, creaking contraption that somehow seems designed to spew dust in faces and pulverize tailbones. It was slow going back up the steep hill and the horses were only moving about as fast as a slow man could walk.

Four men with rifles were upon them with shocking suddenness, and shot the driver and guard before either could react. There were no threats. No demands to toss down the money box. Just quick, matter-of-fact kill shots.

The coach jolted as the horses shied but the team didn't bolt.

The surviving passenger, a banker named Knowlton, was facing forward and leaned out the window and saw a man holding the reins of the front two horses. The man was clearly experienced with teams and managed to calm them in a few seconds.

And then Knowlton was dragged out the window, which on this coach was wide and deep, with the bottom of the window at the same level as the top of the rear wheel.

The man sitting to Knowlton's left was apparently some sort of salesman, judging by the fancy wooden cases he'd had tied on to the top of the coach. Knowlton never got his name, and remembered the man as taciturn, perhaps saving his breath for sales pitches. In fact, Knowlton only remembered the man saying one word the whole trip.

It was *"please."*

But it didn't matter. They dragged him through the opposite window and shot him as he lay in the dust.

Lydia Davis had the rear-facing seat to herself. She was in her mid-twenties and wore expensive clothes, though she did not act like a high-society girl. She had told Knowlton that while she was on her way to visit her father, a judge in Austin, she was not happy about it because, as she put it, her father was an asshole.

The judge had summoned her on some important but undefined request. Maybe the asshole is dying, Lydia had mused to Knowlton.

Lydia didn't seem to mind at all the dirt and dust and smell of sweat that seeps into the pores of the wood and the cracks in the leather seats of coaches everywhere.

She never complained even though she got the worst of the flying grime in the rear-facing seat because the wheels, turning clockwise as the coach moved forward, propelled it in her direction. She had tried drawing the curtain but realized that she could cut down on the infiltration only at the expense of slow suffocation, so she said "fuck it" and took a nap.

The bandits let Lydia keep her seat. Two of the men, dressed like trail hands but wearing bandanas over their faces, carrying rifles and wearing holsters slung low in the style of gunfighters – or men who want to be taken for gunfighters – sat facing her.

She punched one in the nose and so they tied her up.

The other two, also masked, were methodically changing the horses.

They'd brought their own fresh team.

One of the men, a stocky, dark fellow with enormous jet-black eyebrows, asked Knowlton if he had anything to write with. Knowlton had a pen in his pocket and paper in his briefcase and he carefully took down what Eyebrows dictated.

Eyebrows rifled through Knowlton's briefcase, found a business card, read it, and tucked into his breast pocket. He then pointed down the road and told Knowlton to follow it on foot. It would be about a four-hour walk to the stage post, and he advised Knowlton to walk carefully because he didn't want to turn an ankle on such an important mission. But don't dawdle, he warned, because there was no stage scheduled until tomorrow and it was highly unlikely any riders would pass this way, and if he was still walking in the dark it was easy to get lost or fall prey to wolves or both. Sunset was in eight hours.

From the stage post, Eyebrows instructed, Knowlton would arrange transportation to the nearest telegraph office in the town of Twin Ridge and wire State Supreme Court Justice Gates Davis that it would cost ten thousand dollars to get his daughter back alive. Knowlton was to provide Judge Davis with the detailed instructions for paying the ransom.

If Knowlton didn't do as directed, Eyebrows said, the girl would die.

He fished the business card out of his pocket.

And since they now knew his name and work address, Knowlton would also die, Eyebrows added. Along with his family, if he had one. And his dog, if he had one.

With that, Eyebrows hoisted himself up the driver's seat and snapped the reins. He was followed by one other rider who led the horses. They all headed, at a brisk pace, down the road to the spot where the fallen tree had lain.

It was gone now.

A lot happened those ten minutes or so, Knowlton had noted. These people knew what they were doing.

Chapter 12

Harbold asked me to sign a receipt for the money.

"I'm going to have to trust you," I said. "It would take me all day to count it."

"They demanded small denominations. So you've got a thousand greenbacks. All tens."

I never much understood nor trusted paper money. During the war we'd seized property and paid for it with currency that as far as I could determine was an abstract representation of a worthless promise to pay someday, somehow, maybe. Sometimes transactions were made with bank notes, often drawn on banks the receiver had never heard of, and which sometimes didn't exist. I would guess that during and after the war about half the bank notes in the country were phonies.

No one could really tell for sure, except for the cashier at the bank named on the front of the note, and by that time it got that far, if the note were fake it was too late to do anything about it.

The pile of money in front of me now was in "legal tender notes," which were supposed to be good as gold even if they weren't backed by anything except the promise of the government. On these bills it was grandly spelled out on the back in bright green ink that, "Tens notes is a legal tender for all debts public and private except duties on imports and the public debt."

I thought that was a strange way to put things and not quite sure what it meant but Harbold was breathing down my neck – literally, he was an inch in back of me and I could feel his breath – and was clearly anxious to get things in motion.

"Sorry, Sir, but the Major wants this to go off without a hitch. They want to make the trade before sunset and they say they'll kill the girl if you're late."

We had time to ride there twice and back, but Harbold always anticipates the worst and that is a valuable trait in a soldier or lawman, so I signed for the Greenbacks and packed them in a saddle bag.

"I know they say the delivery has to be made by one man alone," Harbold said, "but you could be riding into a deathtrap when you get to that mountain. I can cover you and stay out of sight."

"I appreciate that, but I already planned on having Carmody watch my back. You've got a government job and a nice uniform and a hell of a nice horse, and I don't want you endanger all that if this goes down the shithole because I didn't follow instructions."

"I can live without the job and the uniform. But the horse is another story. Thank you, Sir. For the record, the offer still stands."

"Carmody knows the terrain and kind of blends in. The brass buttons on your fancy uniform might reflect in the sunshine. But what I'd like you to do, if you can, is stay here and mind the fort until I get back. You never know what will happen if there are no lawmen in town."

"Glad to, Sir. Your lady friend invited me to stop by later to see her place and have a drink on the house."

I guess you never know what will happen if there *is* a lawman *in* town, either. But I was due at Table Top Mountain and had to head out.

Chapter 13

Carmody carried the money in his saddlebags. A thousand greenbacks is bulky.

It was actually nine-hundred-ninety-nine Greenbacks and ten dollars in coins. My coins. I'd pocketed one of the Greenbacks, and, not wanting to be accused of being an embezzler, made good on the remainder.

I wanted it as evidence. As evidence of what, I wasn't sure. My gut told me to pocket it, and my gut is usually more reliable than my brain, so I complied.

I didn't carry anything other than a rifle and a sidearm, had no bags on my horse, and wore a tight shirt. I wanted whomever I was meeting to know I didn't have the money on me.

When we met up, they would just have to live with the fact that a third party was dropping the money. We'd work those details out. These were, after all, people who had casually shot three men because their existence was, for the moment, an inconvenience. If I showed up at Table Top dragging bags of money I would be dead as soon as I got within rifle range.

A lot of this would be a seat-of-the-pants maneuver. Assuming I could work out the swap, how I'd survive and get away with a breathing Lydia Davis was something I'd have to improvise.

My options were limited. The notes and directions delivered by the banker were clear: If I came with a posse she'd be dead. If I told the Texas Rangers or an army platoon she'd be dead as soon as they learned I'd issued the alert. The kidnappers told the banker they had ways of knowing such things, and I was in no position to doubt their word. They'd somehow known about the judge's daughter being on the stage, after all, and known that Judge Gates Davis was a man of considerable means.

They'd also known the stage schedule and had exactingly planned the itinerary of the man they'd left alive.

I don't know how they knew all those things. I wished I did.

Chapter 14

I took the main trail to Table Top. I'd never seen the mountain, but Carmody had, and he sketched out a map for me.

The trail paralleled a stream, Carmody said, and then coiled around the base of the small mountain, in actuality more of a big hill. It drew its name from the fact that the top was flat and bald, about an eighth of a mile in diameter, and sat atop a long and gentle upward slope that surrounded it. Table Top was a logical place for a swap of cash for a hostage: Both parties would have to approach each other in the open, and while it wasn't out of the question that a rifleman could find cover to hide behind and hit a rider, Table Top was a wide circle with an open view, and the flat terrain provided maneuverability for a horseman, so if the first shot missed, the second would be much more difficult.

There was only one perch that overlooked Table Top, and that was a rocky peak more than a quarter mile away, well out of rifle range. The summit was about 20 feet higher than Table Top, but inaccessible, as Carmody put it, "to normal people."

Carmody took a higher and much more difficult trail, where there was what you'd call a trail. He had almost complete cover, but the trek wasn't easy. I never could have navigated it, but Carmody can read terrain like you or I read a newspaper. For tracking work, Carmody favors what he calls mountain saddle horses, small chocolate-color breeds that are not particularly fast but are calm and sure-footed and could handle areas as impassible to most horses as they are to us normal people.

The plan was that I'd diagonally climb the north side of Table Top. Carmody would ride as high has he could up the craggy peak and climb the rest of the way on foot. He'd monitor for snipers with his sharp eyes and spyglass and, if the kidnappers really showed up with the girl, drop the money somewhere on the south slope and mark the spot with a branch stuck upright in the dirt so I could find it.

Not a foolproof plan, to be sure, but better odds than if I went by myself with a sack of money and a target on my back.

I lost sight of Carmody about a half-hour into the ride. We would reach Table Top in about 90 minutes, he estimated. There would be no easy way for us to communicate except by firing off a gun in the event of an emergency. One shot meant he would come to me. Two shots meant I'd try to find him if I could.

He also had a small mirror. If the sun came through the clouds he'd use the reflection to signal his presence on the peak.

Again, not a bad plan.

But of course it all fell apart five minutes later when a bullet creased my skull.

Chapter 15

I was aware of my hat flying off before I felt the sting of the bullet.

It was the second time in a month someone had shot my hat off without doing serious rearrangement on my skull. Someone who's not been shot at would think it highly improbable, but I'd seen hats shot off countless times in battle and I was more than a little angry about this one. It was a Stetson model called Boss of the Plains, with a wide round brim, good for keeping the rain out of my eyes, and a sweatband. Elmira gave it to me, and spent a lot of money on it, and I liked it.

Then, as more bullets tore through the leaves, it occurred to me that I had to come to my senses, quit mourning my hat, wipe the blood trickle away from my right eye, and charge toward the sound of the gunfire.

There's only one response to an ambush: You ride or run toward it and shoot like hell while you're in motion. If you run for cover you are playing the ambusher's game, because they would not have tried for the kill had you been near a real sanctuary. If you freeze in place…well, you might as well just shoot yourself and get it over with.

I believed the shots came from behind a cluster of rocks on a ridge above me. I spurred the horse up the slope and felt badly about digging the sharp metal into his flanks, but I'd give him an extra bag of oats later, if there was a later.

My horse is called a Steeldust in that part of Texas because some of its ancestors had a grayish, metallic sheen. Mine didn't, but like all its breed it was still big and exceptionally fast regardless of the fact that the color isn't uniform anymore. Carmody, a connoisseur of horseflesh, had a Steeldust in his stable but had added the small mountain saddle horse to his collection two months ago after a good run at the Faro tables.

The man was a consistently successful gambler. I hoped his luck would hold out today. Mine too.

I and the Steeldust charged.

It's a theory of mine that accomplishments stem from a love of what you do, and the Steeldust was just overjoyed to run flat out, hooves pounding the turf so rapidly you couldn't even detect the rhythmic gap in the pattern when all four feet were off the ground.

Together, we created a cacophony of destruction. I opened up with my seven-shot repeating rifle. It's not easy to shoot a rifle from the hip, and ratcheting it one-handed takes practice, but I'd practiced plenty and could squeeze off a shot every three seconds.

I'd fired three rounds by the time I was within a hundred feet of them, and I saw the first ambusher as he poked his head up and slid his rifle over the top of the rock. He was trying to get the gun to his shoulder and stay low, but in order to look at me, he had to give me a chance to look at him.

I read panic in his expression.

I also think I read his mind. When you plinked at suckers, he was thinking, they were supposed to squeal and run and offer their backs as a nice, broad target.

They weren't supposed to charge their snarling quarter-horse at you and lay down a barrage of big-bore rifle fire.

This was running through his mind as he brought his rifle to his shoulder a split-second before my shot exploded his head, with shards of pristinely white bone flipping through the sunshine amid a billowy spray of pink and red and gray.

Then there were two shots from my right, their left. It was Carmody. I could tell by the boom of that buffalo gun he favored.

I don't know if he'd interpreted the first shot as my signal for help or if he could tell it wasn't the sound of my round, but in any event, he responded like a one-man cavalry and knew exactly what to do.

He'd flanked them.

Nothing scares ambushers more than being flanked, and a second after they'd figured out what was happening they were riding out. They were galloping away before Carmody's shot finished echoing.

Chapter 16

We chased them for a couple miles before we had to give up.

The ambushers had fast horses. Mine was faster, but the ambushers knew the trails and had the advantage of actually being able to see where they were going. My head was bleeding faster than I could wipe the blood out of my eyes, and without the sweatband of my Boss of the Plains hat, there was nothing to impede the trickle.

Carmody's little mountain horse was not much bigger than a pony, and even though Carmody is lean, he's tall and big-boned. I would guess he weighs at least 220 pounds. Even though his mount was unsurpassed at rock climbing, it wasn't meant for long stretches with a heavy rider and it began to blow.

We pulled up and saw them enter the mouth of a what looked like a box canyon. Actually, only Carmody saw them. His eyes are better than mine, but mine are pretty good when they're not covered with a film of blood.

"Shit," I said, wiping my eyes on a sleeve that had become slicked with scarlet and just made the whole mess wetter. I tried my shirt tail and that worked better.

If Carmody were indeed half mountain goat, as rumor had it, some other segment of his genetics might be some species of hunting dog because he is impossible to distract when on point, even when his partner is bleeding out three feet away.

"Are you gonna die like right *now*?" he asked, never taking his eyes off the mouth of the canyon.

"No, but thanks for asking."

"Then give me your horse."

And with that he was gone.

Chapter 17

Head wounds can leak an astonishing amount of blood. The skin is stretched tight and full of veins, I've been told, and when it's cut it splits wide and just spews.

I'd been something of a bleeder when I was fighting. My eyebrows were cut from time to time, usually from headbutts. I never scarred much, though. Some men would thicken up in the eyes and ears and get that forbidding prizefighter look. I was never too worried about the tough-looking ones with the scar tissue, though, because it wasn't so much a badge of toughness as a tell-tale that they got hit in the face a lot.

Because I'd promised Carmody I wouldn't die today, I figured I'd better try to stop bleeding, and soon. I found a stream and let Carmody's horse drink and washed the wound out best I could. The water was moving too fast to provide a clear reflection, but I could half-see and half-feel that the bullet had opened a three-inch gash above my right eye and near my hairline.

I found some white yarrow and crumpled it up. I was never quite sure if it were the flowers or the leaves that were supposed to stanch the flow of blood, so I made a soupy poultice of both and pressed it into the wound.

If the pain of the poultice equated to effectiveness I figured I'd stop bleeding soon, and I did.

I took out my knife and cut off the left sleeve of my shirt and tied it over the poultice and around my head. I pulled it as tight as I could, knotted it, and at some point passed out.

Chapter 18

When I woke up it was dark, but Carmody had a campfire going.

"Damnedest thing I ever did see," he said, as though we had just taken a break in the conversation a minute ago.

I propped myself up on an elbow. I was a little light-headed and faintly nauseated, perhaps from the cloying smell of the dried blood that had caked my clothes. But other than that, I didn't feel too badly.

"What?"

He was turning some meat on a stick over the fire.

"First you got to eat and drink. I filled your canteen; the water in the stream is good. And here's some food."

It took me a second to focus but soon the shape of the meat on the stick suddenly cohered in my mind. I recognized the contour of the haunches, the taper of the body. I could feel the cold horror creep into my bones.

"I'm not eating a fucking squirrel."

"It's a *fox* squirrel," Carmody said, as if the distinction would somehow make a difference.

"Big and meaty," he said. "Native to this area. And I do admit these babies is a mite more tender than the ones back home."

I couldn't tell if the dizziness that overtook me was from loss of blood, the after-effects of the blow to my head from the bullet that had creased my skull, or from watching Carmody bite into what I believe was the thing's horrid little butt.

"We have to get back." I needed to change the subject.

"Traveling at night is tough enough when you're not all passy-out. You need to eat, or you could go paws up again."

"That's all right," I said. "I'll die before I eat that thing. I'd shoot myself. I'd shoot *you* if you wave that under my nose again. I packed some jerky in the saddlebags. From a cow. Not a rat with a fluffy tail."

"I'll get it," he said, mumbling as he walked over to his horse. I could only make out a reference to the fact that *I didn't appreciate nothing* and some random observations on my ancestry.

It occurred to me that he might have a point about resting for the night. I'd only been conscious for about five minutes and already I was seeing twinkling star-showers whether my eyes were open or shut. But Elmira would be worried, and I hated to make her wait until tomorrow afternoon to learn I was all right.

It would be a good idea to get back as early as possible.

And Harbold, who I was counting on to keep the peace and put down any insurrection inspired by one or both of my prisoners, might have to return to Austin if he were wired in the morning.

That made it important to get back.

And Harbold said he was going to hang out with Elmira.

That made it imperative.

So, I heaved myself to my feet, asked Carmody about what had happened to the ambushers, saw a brilliant star-show, and woke up the next morning.

I didn't remember falling down.

Chapter 19

Carmody began his story as soon as we mounted up the next morning.

I was feeling better but was chilled because my clothes were still wet. I'd fallen into the campfire and Carmody had doused me with stream water after pulling me out. There were some burned patches on my shirt and my side stung a little, but I was otherwise in better shape than the local fox squirrels.

"Goddamndest suicide attempt I ever did see," Carmody said as we set out.

"Things always look better in the morning," I said. "Anyway, I'm starting to get my wits back."

I couldn't quite hear his reply, but it sounded something like *such as they is.* I let it pass.

"Anyway," I said, "what happened?"

"You got shot in the head, blew off somebody else's head, and tried to dive into the campfire."

"I know that. I mean after you followed the others who ambushed us."

"And you lost your hat. Kept me awake you delirious and all whining about your fucking hat."

"*Aside* from that. What *happened?*"

"And I don't think Harbold is going to move in on Elmira. You outrank him, and he knows you can beat the shit out of him. Man respects you a lot. I can tell."

"Damn it, Tom."

"Sorry. I'm tiptoeing around telling you what I saw because you probably's going to think I'm making it up."

He had my attention.

"First," he said, poking that finger in the air, "I assume you've come to the same conclusion as me about who the actual target is here."

I hadn't thought about it. I actually hadn't thought about much of anything since getting my hair parted; I'd acted entirely on instinct except for a few moments last night, but my reasoning had been derailed by passing out after I saw Carmody eat squirrel-butt.

But now everything was clear.

"We weren't even halfway there," I said. "And it was obvious I didn't have the money on me. There was never any drop-off planned. Nobody cared about the money. And somebody knew I'd be coming from Shadow Valley. It was an ambush."

"More than that. It was a fucking *assassination.* Set up by somebody who knew you'd been sent on a mission."

My head was clear now. My blood was pumping with an instinctive animal rage and I was thinking about how I'd track down and kill whoever did this.

In other words, I felt pretty good. Everything was back to normal.

"And now," Carmody said, "let me tell you the crazy part."

Chapter 20

There had been two of them, and they apparently did not realize Carmody was tracking. They had cut into the opening of a canyon and worked their way through a narrow passage.

For some reason, Carmody said, they had stopped before the canyon opening and waited for a minute, as though on the starting line for a race, and then bolted into the opening at top speed.

Carmody knew that he couldn't follow directly after them without being spotted, so he'd circled around and found another opening. Most people think box canyons have only one entry point, but very few things in nature are built like that. Carmody found a wormhole to the south, staked his horse, changed to some moccasins he kept in the saddlebag, and walked in, crawling and climbing when he had to.

No ordinary man could have done it. Carmody didn't say that, of course, but the same upbringing that had left him with a taste for homemade liquor and the hindquarters of fox squirrels had imprinted the ability to read terrain, guess the logical way in, remember the way back, and move like a shadow all the while.

He'd drawn on those skills as a Union scout in Tennessee's First Regiment Volunteer Infantry and honed them a little in the process.

He'd worked his way into a deep canyon, darkened by the high walls and narrow opening that blocked out most of the sun except when it was directly overhead. It wasn't a particularly big canyon, but it was deep; the farther you travel northwest the more frequent canyons become until you hit the type of giant gorges you see near Amarillo. The type of formations we have in the Hill Country are smaller and craggier and typically lead to caves. Were you find one cave you'll generally be in one part of a network that leads to other caves and caverns.

Carmody poked his finger in the air and started to explain the differences between caves and caverns but I lost interest – it has something to do with one being bigger and deeper than the other – and I implored him to focus on the topic.

Regardless of which is which, canyons and caves have an understandable attraction to outlaws, especially if the facilities come equipped with limited and complicated access, a perch where the inhabitants can get a view of approaching riders, cave openings or mineshafts that can easily be concealed, and access to water and grass for grazing.

Carmody had spent the afternoon exploring while I was occupied with bleeding and told me that just a few hours northwest of our sleepy little town lay a canyon hideout with all the amenities, essentially a grand hotel of the outlaw world. He estimated during his lurking and skulking he'd seen about twenty men and one woman.

He'd never seen Lydia Davis and neither had I, but she'd been described to us as a sturdy, square-faced young woman with dark brown hair and a stern expression.

Carmody had caught a glimpse of a sturdy square-faced woman with dark brown hair and a stern expression sitting at a rough-hewn table in a low oval-shaped cave, but couldn't get close enough to discern any more. She was shaking her fist and cursing and might have been a captive protesting her plight. Or she may have just been a resident criminal who likes to shake her fist and curse.

She might have been Lydia Davis. But as Carmody told Harbold, she might have been President Grant's wife Julia, for that matter. She sure looked a lot like the picture of Mrs. Grant that Carmody had seen.

Or she could have been any one of a million other people.

But whoever she was, she was somehow a part of the web of events that had culminated in the most recent attempt to turn me into flower food, and we were going to start unraveling this damned business as soon as we got back.

Chapter 21

Elmira screamed when I walked into the Spoon.

"He ain't that ugly," Carmody said.

The tears flowed instantly and copiously. She hugged me and drove her head into my chest and then jerked it back as though to double-check that it was really me and then she burrowed back in again.

It took me a second to figure out her reaction but then I saw myself in the mirror behind the bar. The wound was still open and still had flecks of fresh blood around the edges and gaped like a mouth. My blood was caked into a powdery, coppery brown mess that had cascaded down my shirt and covered it entirely except for the burn-holes. Blood covered my right pant leg but somehow the left one remained pristine.

Harbold rose up from a chair near the Faro table.

"What happened, Sir?" He asked the question in the same tone he'd use to inquire as to whether the mail had come in yet.

Elmira shot Harbold a look of reproach and I couldn't figure out why until I remembered that despite the rough edges of her life she had not seen a lot of blood and did not like the looks of it when she did. When she first hired me, Carmody and I had been forced to do some gunwork at the bar and had pretty much turned the place into a slaughterhouse and she threw up for an entire day.

Some things go unspoken, depending on your background. Harbold, who'd seen just about every type of battlefield casualty that could be imagined – and a few that can't, not by a normal mind, anyway – knew that I was unsightly but not seriously injured. His tone was businesslike because for him and for me, this was business.

Elmira didn't understand that and now she hated him.

Good. I liked it that way.

Harbold listened and wrote in a small notebook he carried in his back pocket.

"Who do you think could have tipped them off?" he asked.

Unspoken, because it didn't need to be said, was any denial on his part.

Elmira was looking at him with ice under her eyelids and I was afraid she was going to say something untoward, but she made a reasonable point when she spoke.

"It could have been any one of dozens of people," she said. "Everybody in town saw or heard about you two riding out, carrying every gun you could lift. You're assuming that this is related to the kidnapping. There are lots of people who want you dead, probably including friends of Mr. Gillis and that judge you've kept locked in a cage for two days now."

"He ain't no real judge," Carmody said.

Harbold interrupted and circled the conversation back to the actual point. "Add to that every drunken cowboy you've whacked alongside the head in the past year. And the people connected to the rival saloon down the street – they may hold long grudges. Lots of people do."

Elmira shook her head.

"But why now?" she asked. "Why wait until they are heavily armed and on the trail?"

"If I had a grudge and wanted to kill the Lieutenant," Harbold said, "that would be precisely when I'd try it."

"I'm not a lieutenant anymore," I said, which went without saying because Harbold ignored me, which he never would have done if we were still in uniform.

"Look," Harbold said, "how exactly do you kill a marshal in the center of town? Without being seen? Much easier if you see him setting off on a trail, regardless of how many guns he's carrying. You know he's riding northwest, and if you know the area you know there are only a few trails headed that way and you set up a perch. That's simple. The only part that isn't so simple is that if it was somebody in town, they would have seen the corporal here ride off, too."

"That's *sergeant*," Carmody said.

"Sorry. But maybe they wanted to kill both of you. Maybe there were more lying in wait on the upper trail. Maybe they saw you and the sergeant and assumed, correctly, that you'd given him all the money to carry. Makes sense that they would pick you off as soon as they could. And maybe it *was* somebody from Austin who knew about the kidnapping and knew you were heading for the drop. The major certainly would have kept quiet about it, but how many people did the judge talk to? And the witness? How many sheriffs and marshals and constables and law clerks and telegraph operators heard some or all of the story?"

Harbold had a way of putting things in perspective.

"So," I said, "that narrows it down to anyone *here* who wants me dead, or who wanted ten thousand dollars, and anyone in *Austin* who wanted me dead or wanted ten thousand dollars, or any combination of the above?"

Harbold nodded.

"So basically, we've narrowed it down to anyone, somewhere in Texas."

"I wouldn't rule out Arizona," Carmody said. "Or the Indian Territories. Or maybe even all of Mexico. The man's got a lot of enemies."

"And just to make it a little more interesting," Harbold said, "we still have the question of Lydia Davis. We promised the major that we'd get her and the major promised that he'd get you out of the frying pan for beating up on that little judge."

Harbold lowered his voice, maybe for dramatic effect and maybe because he was feeling as paranoid as I was.

"And Sir, we don't know who's involved and who's leaking information. If we go after her, it's going to have to be a small operation by people we trust and that no one else knows about. One wrong word picked up by the wrong person and we can tip them off."

Harbold unexpectedly stood up.

"I'm riding back to Austin, Sir. This is a decision for Major Munro. I'll be back tomorrow morning."

And with that he strode out of the bar.

Carmody had fetched a bottle and poured us all a shot.

"If I was you, I'd get a good meal," Carmody said.

"I've lost my appetite for good."

"I'd also have Elmira put some turpentine on that gash."

Elmira looked up.

"You might also want a bath," she said.

"I'll do that. And tonight I need to ride out and see Taza."

"The last time you saw Taza he said he was going to kill you," Elmira said.

"He'll have to get in line," Carmody said, dispensing with the glass and drinking right out of the bottle with those lips that had recently feasted on fox squirrel haunches.

"Refill?" he said, offering up the bottle.

I help up a hand and shook my head.

"I think Taza's promise to kill me was just an open-ended lifetime goal," I said. "Right now I need some information and some help."

"He'd be less likely to kill you if I went along," Elmira said. "We can leave before sundown. After your bath."

I would take her up on her offer. Carmody agreed to stay in town and keep order. I asked him to hide the ransom money. There are lots of loose tongues in down and a big deposit would start them wagging and we had enough trouble as it was.

Carmody assured me he'd bury it somewhere where not even the gophers would dare look for it.

He also concurred that Taza was probably not an immediate threat. As Taza was married to Elmira's daughter, I think Apache protocol would stand in the way of killing me in front of his mother-in-law. Or at least I hoped that was how it worked.

Carmody went to visit the outhouse and I asked Elmira if we could have a fresh bottle and she told me that she would fetch it after my bath.

She stopped be as I swung open the batwing door to leave.

"Josiah," he said, tilting her head. "Where's your new hat?"

Chapter 22

Taza lifted his tunic to show me the scars from our last encounter.

"Here, you make my ribs look like pebbles in stream when you kick me. And here is where knife went in when I fell when you kicked me in leg like little girl does."

I admired my handiwork, administered during a knife-fight between the Apache chief and me when we first met. Carmody and I were caught flat-footed and outnumbered by a party of braves, but Carmody had appealed to Taza's sense of honor and brokered a deal where Taza and I would fight mano-a-mano.

Carmody speaks enough of Taza's language to gather that Taza didn't think I looked like much and I would be easy pickings in a knife fight. On that point, Taza was correct. Taza had me outsized and outclassed with the knife, but he, like most Indians I've encountered, he knew nothing about striking and didn't expect the mule kick that had broken his ribs, nor the windmill shin kick to his thigh I'd learned from a fighter who had picked up the technique in Siam. That's when Taza fell forward, accidentally impaling himself on his knife, and Carmody and I flew out of there like bats at sunset.

A few days later Taza saved my life just as a Comanche was about to finish me off with a rifle shot. Taza did it, he said, so he would have the opportunity to kill me himself at a later date – and take his time doing it.

Taza had surprised me by making that threat in English. He'd played dumb the whole time while Carmody sputtered out the twenty words he knew of the Apache language and Taza pretended he didn't understand us when we were so cleverly plotting against him.

After discoursing on his healing process, Taza told me, "I will not kill you today. Busy with hunting and putting up buildings for storage and winter shelter. Need time to kill you well. Your death will be *delicious* for me. *Delicious*. New word I learn. You know that word? Still think that big dumb Apache cannot speak English? In fact, I know fancy word for big war hero who thinks everybody else is stupid. Word for that big war hero is *stupid*."

I smiled and mused about how much fun I'd have breaking his ribs on the other side.

"I came to ask you a favor."

"To let you die quickly? Not think so, but I make up my mind when I see how hard you beg."

"No, I was hoping you'd risk your life and the lives of a few of your men to go on what's pretty much a suicide mission to help save the life of a woman none of us even know."

"I will do that," he said. "Hunting and chopping trees gets boring."

I explained to Taza that I needed someone on whom I could depend to keep the mission secret. He told me that there was no one he knew to tell, anyway. Then I explained that because we couldn't call in the army or the rangers or any other help because the secret getting out would likely mean the death of the hostage, we would likely be outnumbered, probably by experienced gunfighters. He told me that he welcomed battle and had no fear of gunfighters.

Then I told him about the secret canyon and he told me the deal was off and walked away.

Chapter 23

Elmira gave me an explanation on the way back.

"Taza knows the place and says it's 'bad medicine.' To you and me that sounds like superstition, but it's not, exactly."

I told her I didn't follow.

"It's like last month when you chased that mail thief to Dead Horse Hill. He hid out in a church and you refused to go in after him. What did you think would happen?"

"I figured he'd get tired after a while and give himself up, and that's what he did."

She shook her head and continued in a patient, measured tone.

"That's not what I mean. What did you think would happen if you went into the church? Did you think God would strike you dead?"

I knew where she was going with this and it was an astute observation. Especially coming from someone who believes that the word "gullible" is not in the dictionary.

"No. It's because I believe there are some boundaries you don't cross."

"Why? You're not a particularly religious man, as far as I know."

"It's not that. Because a church is traditionally a sanctuary. You normally don't fire on it in wartime, though it happens. But normally, you set limits because once you bust the limits of decency all bets are off. You can call it a warrior's code, I guess, or the rules of engagement. And yes, it is stupid to think that are rules when you are trying to kill people, but there are traditional limits. They're the last thing that protects civilization."

"And that's your version of bad medicine," Elmira said. "Taza says the place is evil, so evil that it's always in shadow even when the sun is out. It's a canyon hideout, you'd expect it to be dark. And who knows how the idea that the place was evil got cooked up? Maybe it's based in reality. It is an outlaw hideout, after all. Who knows how long it's served that purpose and what goes on in there?"

Again, she had a point.

"Lots of legends and customs get lost in history," I said. "We do things and don't know why we do them. Soldiers salute each other, which is a meaningless action, but at one time it served a purpose: When you were in armor you'd raise your visor to be recognized."

I thought it was interesting, but she was getting bored.

I pressed on regardless.

"We shake hands. That comes from the days when people would hide their weapons up their sleeves, and if you met somebody on the road you'd each feel up each other's sleeve to see if the person you met was armed."

She was riding in back of me as he went single-file through a pass and I couldn't see her eyes. But I think I heard them rolling.

"Getting back to the actual *point,*" she said, "I don't think Taza is superstitious or scared. He just feels some things are objectionable because of his customs and beliefs. You just need to come up with the right way to get him to go along."

She thought for a moment, her brow scrunched up.

"An *incentive,*" she said.

We'd just finished up the half-hour ride from the Apache camp, and were coming up on the trail that would take us to the edge of the delta and turn into the main road near the bank.

I drew on the reins and turned around.

"Would you feel safe riding the rest of the way back by yourself?"

She said yes and waited for me to supply the reason.

"You said the magic word," I told her as I snapped the reins and headed back to the Apache camp.

Chapter 24

I fell asleep as soon as I returned from the Apache camp.

There was a woman whose life was in danger, presumably waiting for me to rescue her, and I suppose I should be riding to the rescue, but reality has a way of getting in the way of good intentions. I had to await Harbold's return and Munro's orders and I was still weak from losing blood.

I wanted to go and I also wanted to stop. I felt like a horse with the bit pulled back and the spurs dug in at the same time.

In war, you confront that feeling pretty much on a constant basis. You know that comrades are in danger fifty miles away but realize that no matter how persuasive the commanding officer may be, an army can't march forever without food and rest. No matter how much you spur it, a horse can only go so far before keeling over. And from a lawman's perspective, there are always people who need rescuing, always troublemakers who need my gun barrel alongside their head, and always predators who need a man with a badge between them and their prey.

I used that line of reasoning to convince my-self that it was all right to go to bed, and slept until dawn when heavy hoofbeats outside Elmira's window woke me.

I looked out the window and realized I was having a dream.

I stood there for another minute and realized I was awake.

Elmira stirred and asked me what the trouble was.

"*Shit.* He's *here.*"

She lay there blinking as I stomped on my boots and jammed on my hat and left, forgetting to close the door.

Chapter 25

His hair was the same white as a decade ago: not an old-man white, although he *was* getting up there, but the shade kids are born with, the type we call towheads because their hair resembles the flax spun to make tow ropes for barges.

The build was the same. So lean you could light a match on him. And the face had a few more wrinkles but still retained its youthful angularity and its patina of tough, utter ruthlessness.

And the voice. The deepest voice I'd ever heard come out of a human, or any other creature, for that matter.

"Thaddeus Munro, reporting for duty," he rumbled. And he saluted.

"Good morning, Major," I said, for lack of anything else. It took me a second, but it occurred to me to salute him back.

"I'm not a major anymore, Hawke, I'm a fucking *state senator*. That trumps a damn *general*. At least in Texas. But right now, you're the boss. Harbold tells me your mountain-man deputy spotted someone who could be Lydia Davis in the Canyon of the Long Shadows."

"That's what the Apaches call it, Major. Senator. I just learned the name yesterday. I asked a chief for help and he turned me down. Told me the place had bad medicine."

Munro raised one of those bushy, coal-black eyebrows that were so out of place against the rest of his pale features.

"You'll have to get back to me on how you got so chummy with the Apaches, but yes, there is 'bad medicine' there. Remember, I grew up around here, on the other side of the Canyon toward Abilene, and we knew about it. Even the wildest kids didn't go near the place, including me. We heard there were holes you'd fall through and things in the air and water that would make you sick. We also heard that outlaws knew a secret way in and used it for a hideout and would kill anybody who tried to make it in."

He paused and we regarded each other silently. I wasn't fully awake yet and it took me a few seconds to take in the big picture.

Munro was mounted on a chestnut Morgan; Harbold's was black. Both men were dressed in civilian garb. Lined up behind Harbold was a string of seven splendid horses, Morgans, Saddlebreds, and a couple of mustangs. Some were laden with thick packs and others bristled with rifles thrust into scabbards, so many rifles that they looked like porcupines.

"These are cavalry horses," I said.

Munro and Harbold nodded. They understood that *I* understood the significance. A top-quality horse suitable for cavalry work could cost upwards of $3,000, and there were damn few of them around after the war. I don't know if anybody will ever figure out a way to count, but I'm sure more horses than men were killed in battle, and replenishing the stock for both species takes time.

A trained horse for battle requires a major investment of time as well as money. The beasts are trained much like soldiers, both physically and mentally. A regular horse can cover maybe 25 miles in a day. One of these could cover 50 and not even breathe hard. Your average horse startles and bolts when it hears gunfire. A cavalry mount ignores battlefield thunder and, if you ask it, will charge right into it.

"How'd you swing these horses, Major?"

"I told you, a state senator trumps a general. Especially when that state senator knows something about the general that the general would not want known by other people, including that general's wife. *Especially* that general's wife."

"Lots of gossip in Austin," Harbold said. "You never know who will really keep a secret, but they trust the Major."

"When I wake up Carmody," I said, "we'll have the only four men in Texas we can trust with what we know."

"I'm up," Carmody said, as usual, from somewhere up on the roof, his favorite venue for keeping lookout. "Been up here for quite some time while you got in your nightly twelve hours of beauty sleep."

"You scared the shit out of me," Harbold said.

"I saw you when I turned the corner," Munro said, beginning to look bored, wanting us to know that spotting Carmody hadn't been much of a challenge. "Harbold described you last night, so I knew it was you. Nice hat."

"I thank you," Carmody said. It came out *ahh thank yee.* "I recently switched to bowlers from derbies. Elegant, but still a good-size brim to keep the rain off."

Munro leveled his gaze back at me.

"I assume you have a plan?"

"I do. Let's put the horses in back so as not to attract any more attention than we have to. I'll make some coffee and take care of the prisoners and meet you inside the bar in ten minutes."

Carmody climbed down from the roof and led Munro's horse through the alley to the back.

"Now, the marshal used to have a beautiful hat," Carmody said as he walked. "Got it shot clean off his head, though. Elmira, woman who owns this bar, his girlfriend sorta like, bought it for him and she's just mad as a mule chewing on bumblebees because he lost it…"

Carmody continued his story as they turned the corner and I couldn't make out the words.

Munro shot me a glance. For the first time since I'd known him, he looked scared.

The prospect of a day spent in the saddle listening to Carmody would frighten any man.

Chapter 26

After Munro, Harbold, Carmody, and I discussed my plan, I went upstairs to roust Elmira. I told her that Munro showed up unexpectedly with a team of cavalry horses and that we had to leave, and had to leave now. I told her to ask Richard Oak, the blacksmith, and Verne Miller, the druggist, to keep an eye on things.

Both men had taken my side during a bank robbery a few months ago. Oak, a young man bristling with muscles and enthusiasm, had shown up with a .22 that wouldn't have felled one of Carmody's fat squirrels at point-blank range. It was Miller, the sour-faced, taciturn old druggist, who'd saved my life by gunning down a robber with, of all things, a musket. The musket had probably hung over his mantelpiece for 30 years, but it sure did the job. Miller had plugged him square in the chest, turned around, and marched home as though he'd just finished mailing a letter.

Elmira does not function well in the morning, and even though she was nodding, I suspected she had perfected a way to sleep while nodding with her eyes open. I was proved correct when she found it impossible to repeat back anything I'd said to her.

I hated to hold things up, but I went downstairs and retrieved a cup of coffee for her and found her snoring. I had to lift her to a sitting position in the bed and close her fingers around the handle of the cup, but gradually she began to regain some of her human-level functions and started nodding again.

"Oak," she said, as though it were a foreign phrase she was trying out the word for the first time. "Miller. All right."

I wasn't sure it was penetrating, but added that she would have to look after Weed and Gillis. Oak or Miller would have to escort them from the cell on an outhouse break and they needed to be fed.

"Weed. Gillis. All right. But I'll ask the nice blacksmith to take care of Mr. Gillis. Miller is *mean.*"

"Mean is *good,*" I told her. "Miller won't be fooled by bluster or sweet-talk. I don't have any idea what Milller's story is – he hasn't said more than a dozen words to me in a year – but he can look after things."

"Look after things," Elmira parroted, the cup tilting dangerously as she began to glaze over again.

I snatched the coffee and left it on the end table. I gave up. Things would have to work themselves out.

When I closed the door, she was snoring again.

Chapter 27

"I realize I am a mere sergeant," Carmody said as we turned northwest. "But has it occurred to any of you officers that we are all crazy?"

"Let's see," Munro rumbled in that voice that somehow came equipped with its own echo. "Hawke here throws a judge in jail, throws anybody who doesn't like what he did to the judge in jail, and to make Hawke's mess go away we agree to save another judge's daughter. Of course, we don't know for a fact it's her. And we're riding into a box canyon to battle it out with a nest of outlaws, even though we're not sure they are the ones who kidnapped her."

"That is correct, sir," Carmody said, "except for the judge part. He ain't no real judge."

"I stand corrected," Munro said.

Harbold spoke up.

"Don't forget that the place is supposed to be haunted. That's the part that I don't like. So, yes, I think we're pretty crazy."

"No doubt about it," Munro rumbled.

"Yup," I said.

"Figgered as much," Carmody said. "Crazy as four rats in a coffee can. Just wanted to make sure we all had the same understanding."

"One thing I actually don't understand," Harbold said, "is that you were ambushed before you were even halfway to the drop-off point for the ransom. Maybe, like we said, they were planning it all along and knew that Sergeant Carmody had the money and were coming for him after they killed you. But coincidences make me uneasy."

"And," Munro said, looking at me, "if the point was to assassinate you, was it a grudge by some local or an assassination orchestrated by somebody who knew about the kidnapping? If it's revenge by a random local, why was Lydia Davis being held in the canyon?"

"We don't know if it's really Lydia Davis," I said.

"I'm pretty sure it's her," Munro said.

Munro was in a few paces in the lead, so I brought my mount up next to him and looked over.

"Why?"

"Harbold told me that Carmody said it could have been Mrs. Grant, because it looked like her. He was joking, but right after Harbold told me I went to see Judge Davis and asked him for a description. There's no picture of Lydia or I would have brought it back to show Carmody. But the part of her looking like Mrs. Grant … well, he confirmed that. In fact, he brought up Mrs. Grant before I did."

"Really," Carmody said. "Kinda, well, *sturdy*? And square-headed?"

Harbold cleared his throat.

"Yes, and from what I hear, pretty head-strong. But at least we know she can ride and shoot. That could come in handy. When she was a teen-ager, she ran away and joined a rodeo."

Carmody's eyebrows were still knitted in concentration. "And would you say she is sort of, you might say, *stern-looking? Maybe a might an-gry-like?"*

Munro nodded.

Carmody looked puzzled for a second.

"And how old is she?"

"Only twenty-six," Munro said.

"Hmmm," Harbold said.

"How about that," Carmody said.

And we rode in silent contemplation for a while.

Chapter 28

Carmody, who has ears like a bat, heard him first.

We could see a dust trail as the rider dipped below the rise, and when we halted our caravan, the *kudulump kudulump kudulump* of a horse in full gallop was just barely audible to me.

We had made no effort to hide ourselves since we left town, and concealing four riders and a trail of packhorses would be pretty much impossible anyway until we got out of open country.

As if on cue, everyone plucked a rifle from a scabbard and spun an about-face with their mounts. Carmody used his left hand to fish a bronze spyglass from his saddlebag.

"Shit," Carmody said. "It's Pickleface."

Munro shot him a glance and then refocused his eyes on the top of the ridge.

"Pickleface, I take it, is a friendly."

"That's a stretch," Carmody said, "but the old sourpuss ain't gonna shoot us. Probably not, anyway."

"His name is Verne Miller," I said. "Local druggist. He keeps to himself, sort of in a *pathological* way, but seems to be drawn to trouble. Last time was at a bank robbery when Carmody and I were outnumbered. Miller showed up with something that looked like a souvenir of the Mexican War and drilled one of them in the chest. Walked away and hasn't said a word to me since."

"He's not carrying nothing today," Carmody said. "He's wearing a holster, but it's empty."

I put my rifle back and heard the metal-on-leather hissing sound of others doing the same.

We waited in silence. Our horses, unlike civilian mounts, tended to remain statue-still when at rest.

Miller said nothing as he reined his mount back to a trot. The horse, a thin creature of unidentifiable breed with flinty eyes, and which bore an uncanny resemblance to its owner, looked spent.

Miller dismounted. He moved briskly for someone his age. I would characterize him as *spry*, but I don't use that word because I'm afraid of the day – if I live that long – that it will be applied to me.

He turned the horse around and swatted it on the rump.

"He can find his way home. I'll ride the silver Morgan. And if you don't mind, I'll use that new German bolt-action tied to her. Don't see many of them out here. Whose is it?"

"Miller," Carmody said, "we ain't taking pills out of big bottles and putting them in little bottles. This is gun-work. This is serious –"

"Here," Munro interrupted. He drew up alongside the silver Morgan. We'd left saddles on all the horses – you never know when one will get shot out from under you and you'll need a spare – even though we'd laden them with packs. He untied the rifle and handed it to Miller butt-first.

Miller worked the bolt with fluid and practiced precision, sighted down the barrel and inspected the mechanism.

"Very methodical people, the Germans. They put a safety on an army rifle. Guess Mr. Bismark doesn't want to waste any bullets."

Miller rooted through a saddlebag and snatched out a cartridge belt. He looked closely at the rounds and knew which one to take.

"Planning on doing some mining?" Miller said, holding up a stick of dynamite. "Nice new formulation. Much more stable mixture than nitro, and a lot bigger bang than powder."

"We'll fill you in," Munro said.

"And I'll need a sidearm. Any single-action will do."

Without asking, he took one out of the saddlebag and slid it into his holster.

"Don't have a revolver myself," Miller said. "At least one that works. I promised myself I'd never wear one again."

Miller stood quietly for a second, contemplating what he'd just said.

"But the biggest lies are the ones we tell ourselves."

I watched with a sense of unreality. Miller had spoken more words in the last minute than in the year or so I'd known him. And now here he was, a sudden apparition in a suicide mission. I needed to figure Miller out, but I was at a loss as to how to start.

Carmody wasn't.

"What the fuck do you think you're *doing?*"

"My part," Miller said as he swung into the saddle. "I have some experience with this sort of thing, and when I saw you riding out I got the story out of the Elmira lady. You're going to need help."

"Elmira *told* you?" I asked.

"She's a talker for sure," Carmody said. "Wouldn't make much of a spy."

"I don't know," Miller said. "Even if you tortured her you'd still have a hell of a time figuring out what she was babbling about. When I finally got her to stick to one subject, she told me you're riding out to Long Shadows to save a girl that had been kidnapped and then something about keeping the marshal out of trouble. I couldn't decipher what came next and let it pass."

"We'll fill you in," Munro said.

I felt irritation swelling behind my eyeballs. I wasn't mad at anyone in particular, except Elmira – who can't help the way she blabs, so getting angry at her is like resenting a duck because it has yellow feet – but I was irritated that everyone else, including Miller, seemed to know about this canyon except me.

Miller apparently read my expression.

"It's not something you'd be expected to know about," he said. "It's an old legend and you're a young man."

I liked the sound of the last part of that and urged him to continue.

"I don't know what your CO has told you about it."

"Only what I heard as a kid growing up toward Abilene," Munro said, his bass sounding a counterpoint to Miller's tenor rasp. "That it's supposed to be an outlaw hideout, and that even the Apaches are afraid to go there because it has some sort of curse or bad medicine or something. I've only seen it once, and then never went in very deep. Gave me the creeps, if you want to know the truth. I felt dizzy and sick."

"Same here," Miller said, piping into the flow of conversation like a badly played, raspy oboe. "I went in three times, when I was a kid. Used to live about on hour south. It was Yellow Fever country – still is – but Yellow Fever doesn't make you sick in an hour, so that couldn't be it. But *something* got to me."

"What else do you know?" Munro asked.

"Well, I never saw it, but I heard tales of flash fires out of nowhere. People just burned up sudden-like. But that was fifty years ago. Never heard people talk about it until now. The Elmira lady says the deputy here rode in and spotted outlaws and the victim."

"I didn't ride in," Carmody said, still giving Miller the sideways glance he sometimes subjects me to when he doesn't believe what I'm saying or just wants to get on my nerves. "I rode around the other side and found a trail to walk and crawl in. Didn't get sick or burned up though."

"That's how you're going in this time?" Miller asked.

"No," Carmody said. "Frontal assault. You men couldn't navigate the climb."

Munro cleared his throat, sort of a volcanic, phlegmy rumble of disapproval.

"No offense meant, Major," Carmody said, but I wasn't convinced he wasn't getting in a gratuitous dig.

"We have to listen to Carmody," I said. "He understands terrain better than any man I've ever known and if he says we can't get in, we can't."

"And if we climb and crawl in, we sure as hell can't get the lady out, if we are lucky enough to find her," Carmody said.

"Good point," Miller said. "So we go in and out the front door. I assume you've come up with a way to do that without getting killed."

Harbold was getting impatient.

"We've got a four-hour ride to give you the details," he said. "And we don't know if you should come along. No offense, but if you slow us down or screw up, it's our lives on the line. You said you had some experience in things like this. What's that mean?"

"That's my business," Miller said. There was no anger in his voice. Just a matter-of-fact statement of what he considered plain fact.

Harbold wasn't angry, either. He knew, better than most, that a man sometimes wants to keep his past his own property.

"Whether you come along," Harbold said, "is a decision that's up to the senator."

Miller sniffed. "Who the hell is the senator?"

"I mean the major. He's also a senator."

"But I'm not a major anymore," Munro said.

"*Damn* it," Carmody said. "Everybody here has two names and three titles."

Carmody turned to me.

"Lieutenant Marshal, or Marshal Lieutenant, or Your Highness, or whatever you would like to be called, for the rest of this trip may we just dispense with the titles and call each other by our names? It might be helpful to us when we're getting our asses shot full of holes to be able to figure out who's who."

"OK," Harbold said. "*Anything* to get this show on the road. Call me Tom."

"That ain't gonna work," Carmody said. "I'm Tom too."

"Oh, for Christ's sake, then I'm *Harbold.*"

"And I'm Carmody."

I shrugged.

"I'm Hawke."

"All right, I'm Miller."

And then he snapped the reins and, without waiting for permission, began the procession to the Canyon of the Dark Shadows.

"*Captain* Miller," he added, softly, speaking to no one in particular.

And that was all he would say on the subject for the rest of the trip.

Chapter 29

Even though we'd dropped the honorifics, Munro remained in charge. We agreed on that. Among other qualifications, Carmody noted, Munro had a hell of a loud voice.

Carmody would be the first into the canyon. He had the best eyes and had some recent familiarity with the territory. We'd follow him to where we thought Lydia Davis was being held.

Munro would ride in next. He would order me and Harbold to fight or scout according to how he sized up the situation.

Miller would cover us from the rear. He would also lead us out when and if we snatched Lydia.

As we came over the final rise I saw Taza and some braves on horseback.

They were there to provide the grand finale.

The last quarter mile, only path into the canyon, was totally exposed. We had to assume we were being watched, and assume we'd be spotted, and therefore there was no point in trying to sneak in.

Still, there was no point in making a lot of noise and calling attention to ourselves.

So after we ground-hitched the spare horses, Munro kept his voice low when he gave the order to charge.

Chapter 30

The first thing you noticed was the smell. It was a mixture of rotten cabbage, dead buffalo, and moldy basements.

Then it became dark during a brilliant Texas mid-day. The walls were steep, and the sky was reduced to a narrow, jagged bolt overhead.

And then I got lightheaded.

Carmody shook his head like a dog – you could hear it flopping – and glanced backward. We were still in tight formation and he was only two lengths ahead of me.

Harbold looked over at me.

"What the fuck is this?" he said. "Poison gas?"

"Keep moving!" It was Miller. His voice retained its oboe honk but now seemed to carry a ring of command.

"Now that I smell it again, I know exactly what this is," Miller said. "I was an engineer before the war. It's *swamp gas*. There's a backed-up stream to the right and no ventilation or air movement at all because of these high walls. This rock formation traps the gas. The gas itself won't hurt you, but it keeps you from getting air."

We'd slowed the horses to a canter because we couldn't see well in the gloom.

"Will it clear up?" I asked.

Carmody pointed ahead.

"The canyon has to open up soon. What I saw from the other side was a lot wider. Press on and hope we make it. Can't be more than a few hundred feet."

My mount stumbled a little. Horses, even cavalry mounts, stumble on rocky terrain all the time. But under the present circumstances, it made me worried.

"Miller," I said in a burst, trying to save my air, "will it affect the horses?"

"I said I was an engineer, not a veterinarian. How the fuck would I know?"

We rode on and I began to see little gray sparkles in the corners of my eyes.

"Miller, should we hold our breath?"

"Use as little air as you can. Start conserving it by shutting up with all these questions."

Munro pulled up alongside Carmody.

"It opens up in fifty feet," his basso profundo resonating in the small chamber. "We'll have plenty of air. But we'll also be exposed. If they're going to start shooting, it'll be as soon as we see sunlight."

The man knew his business. As we charged into the open, I got my hat shot off for the second time in one week.

Chapter 31

Even though the canyon had opened up it was still a tight bowl, and the echo made it impossible to locate the source of the shot.

Munro was the first to see the tell-tale smoke, and he opened up on the shooter.

The shooter was now Munro's business, and we let him handle it. Each of us knew not to get distracted by the first shooter because there would inevitably be more.

Carmody was up on his stirrups when he saw the glint of the gun-barrel behind some rocks on the right-hand side of the bowl. I saw it too, and we both twisted and fired.

It's not easy to fire a rifle from horseback because you have to maintain your balance and sometimes, if you're keeping the stock on your shoulder and aiming with one eye, you have to twist your body as much as 90 degrees. That's harder than it sounds, but once you learn the technique, it gives you the advantage of using the superior firepower of the rifle over a handgun.

We both missed but were each able to get off a quick and steady second shot because the horses were completely gun-broken. Teaching a mount not to react to gunfire can take upwards of six months, but in combat it's worth every minute of the effort. Our horses were rock-solid and our second shots were dead on target. The gunman's head exploded in a burst of gore and his shiny revolver spun out of his hand down the hill.

Miller started firing from the rear. I could hear the clicking of the bolt and the unusually high-pitched crack of the German rifle. I wasn't sure if he were aiming at gunmen or just laying down cover fire. In the long run it didn't matter because we had guns and bullets to spare. If we lived through this, I thought, we could open a gun store.

But for now, we were in a bad spot. The bowl was like a theater or an operating room, with seating almost encircling us, all with clear lines of sight for the outlaws' shooting pleasure. Having said that, the vegetation was low and there weren't many rocks, so we had a pretty good view of them, too. And although we were caught in a crossfire, our targets were elevated, so for the time being we didn't have to worry about shooting each other.

All we could do was fan out so as not to present a concentrated target, pick off whoever we could spot, and follow Carmody in whatever direction he felt would lead to Lydia.

Munro and Harbold were opening up at gunmen nested in the sides of the hills. I saw three men leave their positions and break for the top of the rise. They hadn't expected this. Victims were expected to clutch in a panicky knot while you picked them off from your elevated perch – not fan into formation and blast back with rifles.

The gunmen were each about fifteen feet from the rim of the bowl, and I could see two more snipers lying flat on the rim. It was not an ideal perch because they had no choice but to be partially exposed. A man lying level with you can sink into the grass and shoot up from almost complete cover. Here, the snipers had to look down and expose their heads when they leaned over.

"Carmody," Munro bellowed, pointing, "take those snipers."

Carmody took aim, zeroing in for an uncomfortable amount of time. Bullets were buzzing by him, and me, but I don't think the shooters were practiced – they'd given that much away by taking up a bad position to begin with – and were undoubtedly distracted by Miller's cover fire. I assumed Carmody was banking on the notion that two perfect shots were worth the risk of taking time to set them up.

I didn't have time to watch as I had my own business to deal with. I opened up on the shooters running up the hill. They ducked and ran in jagged spurts that they thought would make them hard to hit.

There was no way to tell who hit whom as they scrambled in what were perfectly predictable patterns and conveniently ran into our line of fire as we led them by a pace or two. I believe I hit all three. I'm sure Munro, Harbold, and Miller all felt the same way.

Carmody's rifle cracked twice while I was firing, and when I looked up I could see one sniper lying outstretched, apparently lifeless, with his rifle more than an arm's length away. The other was clutching the rifle on one hand and his side with the other while struggling to get to his feet.

There was another crack from Carmody's rifle, but I ignored it and turned back to surveying the bowl. I was sure Carmody's second shot would be on target, and playing spectator could get me killed.

I'd lost track of how many shooters we had cut down. Normally I'd keep count, but because we didn't know how many there were in total it didn't matter. There could be none left. Or there could be a hundred.

The only way to tell would be to follow Carmody through the next pass to get to the grotto where Lydia Davis was supposed to be held captive. The pass was steep and sheltered by trees and a narrow rock pass. It looked safe, but probably opened up into a new shooting gallery. I had a feeling whoever had escaped this aborted ambush would be there, at the next staging ground.

Instinct told me that for the moment we weren't going to be shot at. Stage one of the battle was over; they'd retreated to the next staging ground.

I looked at Carmody. Instead of heading to the pass he pointed to a rock next to a fallen tree. A gun came spinning out from behind the rock and two quivering hands eased up gradually but fitfully were drawn back down, as though the man behind the rock was afraid of getting them shot off.

Chapter 32

In a different time decades ago, in a now-foreign environment of books and slate boards and chalk, I'd been adamantly opposed to torture.

My younger self would have said the practice is wrong according to basic moral reasoning based on principles that exist in nature. And if the practice is wrong in theory it's *always* wrong. Even if you invent right-sounding justifications it still *has* to be wrong, because if you can concoct your own excuse for breaking a moral code, there's no sense in having a moral code to begin with.

The war and my ten years or so as an itinerant lawman didn't make me less moral. Just the opposite, I think. Experience has just made me more aware that sometimes you have to trust that doing what you would normally classify as the wrong thing can produce a greater good.

The decision about whether to torture the guy with the huge, bobbing Adam's apple we'd captured was further complicated by the fact that time was very limited. We didn't have time to light our pipes and stroke our beards and think abstract thoughts about right or wrong. We believed a woman's life was at stake, and so were ours. Every second we delayed gave the enemy time to mass and plan a new attack.

There are two types of torture. The first is that you cause somebody pain and promise to stop when he tells you what you need to know. In addition to the inherent moral dilemma, there's a practical issue involved in this strategy because people will say anything, including outright fabrication, to stop the torment.

Alternately, you say you're going to do something to him that's permanent, like cutting off an ear, and give him one chance to tell the truth. If he doesn't talk, or if you don't believe what he says, you'll do the deed. If you're convincing enough, you'll often get the whole story without having to do anything besides make threats.

Munro employed a combination of both methods with a suddenness and brutality that made me uncomfortable. Carmody, who possessed no reluctance to cuff a bad guy around when necessary, has some feelings about battlefield ethics and seemed both shocked and sad when Munro, without preamble, shot Adam's Apple in the knee.

The man fell to the ground and screamed, flopping and twisting in the dust, the scream increasing in intensity as the shock wore off and the pain intensified.

"A man can get along fine with one knee," Munro said. "Maybe a limp, possibly a cane, but you'll get around fine. But no knees is a different story. That's a life in a wheelchair. And that's if you don't die out here because you can't crawl back."

Munro stepped closer.

"I can't miss from this distance, no matter how much you flail around."

Miller was the lightest, probably weighing only about 150, so we tied the sobbing Adam's Apple to his horse and they rode double. Miller took the lead. We didn't believe for a second that anybody in this canyon would hold their fire to save Adam's Apple, but with our prisoner positioned on the mast of the ship, so to speak, he had an additional incentive not to lead us into a trap.

We reloaded and prepared to meet the remaining men and extract Lydia Davis from the second cave on the right.

I thought about retrieving my hat, but it was just a cheap old one so I didn't much care. Anyway, I had a couple spares back at the office, even if they were more embarrassingly ragged that the one I'd just lost.

Chapter 33

We didn't dawdle. The element of surprise was gone, but there was no point in giving them more time to prepare.

None of us, of course, had any idea what to expect beyond the next pass other than what Adam's Apple had howled out to us: A rock wall on the right with the opening to three caves, the second of which held Lydia and was large and deep enough to be called a cavern. It struck me that even Adam's Apple could articulate the difference, but I was still confused.

Beyond the cave openings lay another grassy, bowl-shaped clearing where horses and livestock were kept, according to Carmody's scouting, and after that were more steep canyon walls that closed into a box and offered no exit except for a steep and narrow crevice up the side, a trail that Adam's Apple had assured us was impassible. Carmody nodded to me, confirming that the crevice was indeed the trail; he'd somehow managed to do it.

There were supposed to be ten men left, Adam's Apple had warbled.

Now I'd need to start keeping count of how many we killed.

Chapter 34

"Hawke, scout to the left," Munro shouted as we thundered through the pass, the horses as close as they could be to each other without touching. It was a surreal journey, with men and horses bobbing in the dusky light, the thudding of hooves pounding like cannon-fire as the din echoed in the confined space.

I kept my eyes focused on the distant glow of the exit, not so much to keep pursuing it as a destination – the horse could figure that out – but to keep my eyes from getting accustomed to the darkness and being blinded when we burst into the partial sunlight. We knew there were caves on the right. We were not sure who or what was on the left, and it was my responsibility to identify and counteract any threat from that direction.

A few seconds later, blinking but forcing myself to look even though the brightness hurt, I observed that the territory on the left was a stepped terrace where the water that had once run through here had cut away the rock formation into a series of ledges. Most of the wall was too steep for an ambusher to climb or gain a purchase, but parts of the slope were gentler for the first twenty feet or so. I could see one or two spaces where a hostile could have climbed and secreted himself. I couldn't tell for sure, but farther down there appeared to be a depression where a man could flatten himself and hide from view.

I spurred the Morgan and tore down the left-hand side of the passage as close to the wall as I could safely ride. There was no point in giving an ambusher distance to aim; if someone was hidden against the wall, I'd be on top of him in an instant and he wouldn't be able to draw a bead.

The nice thing about having plenty of guns and ammo is that you can fire indiscriminately, so I did. Knowing that I was headed for close action, I'd scabbarded the rifle and fired a double-action Colt with my left hand. One of the things Munro had drilled into us was the notion that if you practice, you can do anything as well with your left hand as with your right, and vice-versa if you're naturally left-handed.

I fired into each potential hiding spot, looking back as I passed.

Gunfire erupted to my right, but that was not my concern at the moment and not my assignment, so I ignored it.

Potential hidey-holes one and two were unoccupied.

The narrow outcropping, the spot where I thought an ambusher could flatten and conceal himself, was a few feet ahead.

He was armed with a rifle, and as I expected was pressed flat against the wall.

He probably expected that I'd be an easy target. It would have been a simple matter for him to turn, lean out from behind the outcropping, and fire on me. The problem with his plan, though, was the thousand-pound cavalry horse bearing down on like a runaway train.

He tried; I'll give him that. The gunman moved as quickly as he could. He swung the rifle out an instant before I was upon him and didn't even get it halfway to level before I dropped the reins, reached out, and snatched the barrel it with my free hand. The rifle tore out of his grip and fired in the air. The barrel scalded my hand. I dropped it and turned on the attacker.

Carmody, who has a way with colorful backwoods dialogue – which I think he actually studies and memorizes, probably writing it down in a secret file to trot out while holding forth at the bar – says an agile horse can stop on a dime and give you nine cents change.

The ambusher knew what was coming when he saw the smartness with which the mount turned on him. But he gave it one last try: His fingers had almost reached the butt of his sidearm when I shot him in the forehead.

I made a mental note. *Nine left.*

For the first time I looked to my right and didn't like what I saw.

There were, indeed, three cave openings. The one in the middle was taller than it was wide. On either side, maybe sixty feet in each direction, were two other openings that were smaller and had narrow, low arches cut into the rock-face. They looked like puckered, toothless mouths.

Sickly trees and bushes sprouted in front of and beside the openings. Not a lot – just enough to provide possible distraction cover for a moving hostile. In combat, you learn to hide behind anything if you need to. Even a tree the size of your forearm can provide just enough distraction to throw your attacker's aim off.

Because of the complexity of the landscape, it took us a few seconds to figure out where the shots were coming from. Some emanated from the mouths of the caves, judging by the strange dampening of the sounds.

But there was gunfire from above.

"Shit," Carmody said as he fired.

I looked up and added my observation.

"Shit."

Some bunch of bastards – either the present collection or a different group from some time in the past, maybe the Stone Age, for all I know – had actually carved out inlets in the mountainside. Maybe they'd been dwellings at one time. They were connected by narrow ledges, and for all I knew there could have been access from somewhere in the rear.

But my job had been to clear the enemy from the left, and I had, so I shouted it out.

"Then hug the right wall," Munro said. "Carmody and Harbold, stay in the center and fire up at the ledges."

Munro made a good choice. Harbold and Carmody were probably the best rifle shots among us. Munro knew of Harbold's eye from observing him in combat, and I'd told Munro that Carmody could shoot the stars out the sky on a cloudy night, which may in fact have been a phrase I'd borrowed from Carmody.

It was an odd time to realize that I'd started talking like him, but I comforted myself with the fact that I'd probably caught it in time.

Meanwhile, Miller was exchanging gunfire with someone inside the first cave. Whatever round Munro had packed for that German rifle Miller had taken a fancy to carried a wallop. We could hear the screaming ricochets from inside.

Adam's Apple was still tied to the horse, sitting directly in front of Miller. Miller had him by the hair and pulled him upright, using him as a shield.

Adam's Apple pleaded to his comrades in arms.

"It's *me*," he shouted. "Don't shoot. It's *me.*"

And with that, somebody shot him in the chest and he slumped forward.

Miller swore and held the back of his left hand against his side. When he withdrew it, he noted the smear of crimson. The bullet had passed through the center of Adam's Apple's chest but only grazed Miller. Bullets take crazy turns inside a body, bouncing off this and that; I've seen a round hit a man in the hip and travel down the entire length of the thigh and lodge in a kneecap. Luckily for Miller, the bullet that killed Adam's Apple took a zig and emerged at an angle that tore a slanting gash in his shirt and cut just deep enough to start some blood flowing.

"Asshole," Miller screamed in his piercing oboe voice, and grabbed what by now was probably the corpse of Adam's Apple by the hair and yanked him upright. Miller spurred his horse and his human shield into the mouth of the cave.

"Get flat against this wall," Munro barked. "Right next to me."

It took a second, but we coaxed the horses into pasting their sides against the wall between the first and second cave opening.

You hear and read about officers being "brilliant strategists" and the like, and in the abstract it sounds like praise for a clever chess player. But you only begin to understand the depth and significance of a strategy when it saves your life. I'd been caught up with the snipers from above, and Miller's charge into the cave and hadn't absorbed what Munro always called "the overall."

The overall, in this case, was that with us hugging the wall near him, a part where the rocks tapered inward just a few inches, the snipers from above would have to lean over the edges of the trails and inlets to fire down at us.

It was just a matter of inches, but life and death is often a matter of inches, or fractions of an inch.

Three men poked their heads over just far enough so they could see, scuttled forward a little more in order to give themselves room to brace their rifles against their shoulders, and immediately died.

I killed one with my rifle butt resting on my thigh and the barrel pointed upward. It was a strange position from which to shoot, but it's hard to aim directly overhead with the butt on your shoulder.

The next couple minutes were like one of those carnival shooting games where metal outlines of heads and shoulders pop up in different locations. I never played that game but had a hunch I'd be good at it, because picking them off above my head was no challenge at all.

Munro's mind was on the next maneuver.

"Carmody," Munro said, "cover us from the fire above. Harbold, you cover anything from the mouths of the caves in that direction."

Munro pointed theatrically.

"That direction," he said, and pointed again.

Harbold nodded and positioned his mount.

You had to admire Munro's command abilities, irrespective of how you viewed his penchant for casual brutality.

I'd seen men die in combat because an officer screamed *left* or *right* when everybody was scrambling in different directions and had no common reference. Or they didn't know if they were supposed to move to *their* right or the *commander's* right.

Now we knew exactly where Harbold was aiming, and it was a perfect strategy. Harbold would be facing away from us, but he had caves two and three, of which we knew nothing concerning potential occupants, covered. If there were in there, they were pinned. Anyone so much as poking their head out would be target practice. Of course, that could include the woman we'd come to save, so Harbold needed to maintain a sharp eye and quick judgment.

Carmody fired off a couple more shots and then yelled out a warning.

"Watch out above."

I jerked my head and rifle upward, but the threat wasn't from gunfire. A body thudded into the dust just a few inches from me, but not before his boot caught me on the shoulder and another slapped into the horse's withers.

I swore and grabbed where it hurt. The horse, who apparently had been better trained than I, remained stoic.

Carmody hollered again.

"More coming. It's *raining* outlaws."

Another man pinwheeled by, a gruesomely choreographed swirl of arms and legs, and he landed in front of us with a nasty crunch. A split-second later his rifle hit butt-first and discharged, as cocked firearms are wont to do on impact with the ground. And then his hat fluttered down.

In a macabre bit of animism, his hat landed neatly on his chest.

I looked up again and could see a head and arm hanging over a ledge. This shooter was not going to fall. He wasn't going to shoot again, either, because half his head was missing.

I heard the creak of leather and glanced over to see Carmody struggling to right himself in the saddle. The stray shot when the airborne rifle hit the ground had caught him in the left arm and twisted him around, so far that he almost fell; he somehow held his rifle and the rim of the saddle pommel as he struggled to pull himself back up.

"Cover *above*," he snapped, irritated that I was looking at him and not the threat from the sky. He had a point.

"Hawke is covering above," I yelled. "Carmody's down."

"Carmody is fucking well *not* down and is back to covering above," he said. "Tend to your own business now."

My business was cave number two, reputed to be the temporary home of Lydia Davis. All I knew of the inside is what Carmody had relayed to me after a glance of only a few seconds. It was arch-shaped, with a flat floor and swirling patterns carved into the rock walls. The ceiling reached a height of maybe fifteen feet at the top and the room stretched back a considerable distance, perhaps sixty feet. Carmody was not able to tell if there were openings at the back that led to other passages.

The cave, Carmody told me, had been lighted by candles and lanterns.

If indeed there were kidnappers in there, unless they were extraordinarily stupid they would have extinguished all light by now. Presumably they had their weapons in-hand already, and understood that we would be at a considerable disadvantage entering the cave if we were framed in daylight and they lurked in darkness.

And just to make things more difficult, we couldn't go in there shooting blindly because the whole purpose was to come back with an intact and unventilated woman.

And that's where Miller came in.

But right now he was occupied. Miller was inside cave number one and there was gunfire echoing inside.

Chapter 35

Munro held up a hand.

I wanted to go in after Miller. Obviously, Munro thought differently.

"Hawke, there's nothing to be gained by riding in. If Miller rode into a deathtrap, then he's dead and there's no point in winding up the same way. If he can get out, he will, but we'll just get in the way if we clog up the mouth of the cave."

"Damn it," I said, "he's an old man."

Munro shot me a hard glance and it occurred to me that he and Miller were probably about the same age. It seemed an odd occasion for Munro too take offense, but vanity has no boundaries.

"Old men are *smart,*" Munro said. "And *mean.* Those are qualities that come with age, so right now I give him the advantage. I think he'll be out any minute."

As if on cue, an oboe voice from inside shouted, "I'm coming out alone."

Miller *was* smart. I'd already known about the mean part.

If Miller had ridden straight out without warning, we'd have had no idea whether it was him or a hostile and he could have gotten shot by accident. And by letting us know he was alone, he freed us to cover other threats rather than bracing for an attack from his pursuers.

Maybe Munro was right about old-man smarts. I hope so. It'll give me something to look forward to.

Miller burst through the opening. He and the horse had to duck below the overhanging rock, and when the mount straightened up, the upper body of Adam's Apple jerked upright and the back of his head smacked Miller in the mouth. Miller shoved him forward and told the dead body, without irony, to stay the fuck out of the way.

Carmody had done an outstanding job tying the man in front of the saddle. Those country boys really know their knots.

"There were two in there," Miller said. "Accommodating hosts. Left the lights on for me."

"Hug the wall," Munro said, and Miller understood and complied.

"If this guy told us the truth," Miller said, pointing to the body slumped in front of him, "there are three or four men left."

I took a look and listen. There was no active firing. No sounds of scurrying. No glints of metal in the jagged sunlight.

Carmody continued to scan the outcroppings. He looked pale, though, and his left arm hung limp and looked as though it had been dipped in bright red paint up to the shoulder.

Harbold kept his rifle trained on a line running in front of caves two and three.

"I'm not optimistic about this guy telling us the whole truth," I said, lowering my voice. "He had to tell us the truth about the caves because we'd see for ourselves soon enough, and if he lied, who knows what body parts Munro would shoot off. But we have no way of knowing how many more might be lurking in this complex. Come to think of it, lying would have been in his best interest because we'd get overconfident."

Miller grabbed a handful of hair and lifted the head.

"Lying asshole," he said, and shoved the head forward into the horse's mane.

"If the cave you just shot up is empty except for the men you just killed, let's try to blow the mouth shut," I said. My plan was to seal the caves so hostiles couldn't retreat back into them, or, if they connected with passages from the rear, enter from some subterranean passage and ambush us.

The dynamite had posed a powerful temptation. As appealing as it was to toss explosives back into the caves and kill everyone before entering, we knew we'd have no certainty as to where Lydia was, or if there were someone else besides hostiles in the caves, perhaps held there against their will.

But my goodness, did we have enough dynamite to blow things up in a big way. Harbold knew a supplier and brought enough of the stuff for us to start our own mining company.

"Let me do it," Miller said. "All right?"

I don't know why I hesitated. All Miller wanted to do was blow the mouth shut, but I have mixed feelings about explosives.

I had very little exposure to them during the war. Once, I'd seen troops throw black-powder grenades that looked like fat, overgrown darts. The needle on the front was supposed to trigger a percussion cap that would blow the whole thing up but it often failed to detonate, and occasionally the things would be thrown back at us.

The Rebs had used bombs buried in the ground. We called that type of bomb "torpedoes" and generally thought of them as barbarous. That's one of the contradictions of war: While it may seem strange to some to cast moral judgments on the means of killing when the whole point of the exercise is to kill, even the most hardened soldier at least has second thoughts about some methods of warfare.

I didn't like torpedoes. It always struck me that indiscriminate killing ran against some innate streak of decency.

Taking a fort by invasion, for example, always seemed more decent an act than burning it down, even though I can't articulate exactly why, even though in the time before I became a soldier, my business was trying to explain things like that.

On the other hand – and that's the damn problem, problems like this have more hands than centipedes have legs – is it right to lose lives on your side when there is an efficient way to kill those who you know will kill you and your allies?

All of us confront the issue of how far we'd go. Would I shoot a man in the knee to get life-saving information? Would I, like the 14th-century Mongols, catapult a body infected with the plague over castle walls and wait for the inhabitants to die?

"*Hawke*," Miller said, the oboe-drone insistent, snapping me back to the moment, "can I do it or not?"

I spoke quickly, surprised at how I'd frozen.

"Sure. Just light it and toss it a few feet in, I guess."

Miller shook his head as he fished out two sticks and a tin of matches.

"That'll accomplish nothing. All the energy will be dissipated front and back. You need to wedge at least two sticks into crevices."

Munro edged his horse over and cleared his throat.

"Gentlemen, we are in an enemy stronghold and possibly surrounded by gunmen who are sighting on us at this moment. Could we discuss physics later, over a beer, maybe?"

Miller dismounted, placed the charges, and was back on his horse in no more than ten seconds.

"If I were you I'd move twenty feet toward the middle cave," Miller said. "I've never used these new fuses and they—"

I felt as much as heard the blast. The rumble of the sound slapped me first, and then came a rush of air.

"...burn quicker than I expected," he said, shaking his head and brushing the dust off his shoulders.

The mouth of the cave had not been completely sealed, but enough debris had been blown down that it would take a man considerable and time-consuming effort to crawl through.

The sudden quiet was unnerving because I could hear a whistling in my ears and wondered if I'd jarred something loose in my head.

There was not a lot of time to think, but I paused and took stock. We were still alive, and that was good. But any hope for a surprise rescue had disappeared at the start of a protracted gun battle that continued noisily for five minutes and had just culminated in a brain-jarring explosion.

The threat from above had, for the time being, been neutralized, up and until the time when they figured out they could drop rocks or boiling oil or something on us without having to expose themselves.

We had no idea who was in cave three, but Harbold could comfortably pick off anybody who ventured forth.

Cave two ostensibly held our target and an unknown number of bad guys. There may or may not be bad guys remaining above. And beyond the next pass lay uncharted territory where for all when know there could be a regiment of bad guys massing at this moment.

I'd had too much experience in this sort of thing to be drawn into any sense of security. A novice to battle might expect that the opposition had shown all its cards by now, but things play out differently in the real world. Now, to us, it seemed as through we'd been shooting all day. But probably no more than ten minutes had actually passed, and ten minutes goes by pretty quickly if you're caught by surprise and planning a counterattack. It takes time to figure out what's happening, grab your gun, get dressed if you need to, confer with your allies, and gather together a group and devise a plan.

Chances are whoever was left – whether it be three, thirty, or three hundred of them – were back there right now, drawing plans in the dirt with a stick. Any survivors of the gun battle were now regrouping and confronting the reality that they were dealing with some hard men.

And we still had the problem of cave number two. We'd heard nothing from inside, but why should we? Anyone in there had no immediate prospect of gain by exposing themselves or giving away their position; just the opposite was true.

But now the balance of power had tilted. We'd won the first round and were in a position to storm the center cave. In fact, we *had* to. Time was now on their side.

We knew that.

Chances are, they knew it too.

And, of course, they did.

"I've got a gun pressed right to her temple," said a voice from deep inside the cave, oddly muffled by distance and at the same time given a sharp edge by the echo of the hard-rock chamber.

Then we heard a female voice. But it was deep. Really deep. In music it's called a contralto. Contralto voices have great carrying power and clarity, and we could make out every word as clearly as if she were speaking from a pulpit.

"You can't shoot me, asshole. I'm assuming they're here for me, and if you kill me, there's nothing to stop them from killing you and the other two guys."

Munro raised his eyebrows.

"I am *impressed*," Munro whispered. "She's got a gun to her head but has the presence of mind to tell us there are no other friendlies in there and that there are three hostiles total."

The contralto rang out again.

"And when I get out of here I'm going to shove that gun up your scrawny ass."

"I am *very* impressed," Munro said, nodding.

Chapter 36

Again it became church-like silent, except for the remnants of that whistling noise in my ears.

And then Carmody heard something. He hears things other people can't, and when he does, he has a habit of tilting his head like a dog, first to the left, then to the right.

"Permission to scout through the next pass," he whispered to no one in particular.

'Do it," Munro said. "Keep hugging the wall and ride right in front of the opening to the third cave. Nobody inside can react that fast to shoot you. Then cut to the left so Harbold has a clear shot at anybody who pokes his head out. I'll watch the ledges above."

Carmody nodded and was off like a foxhound.

Munro talked to me while he looked up, squinting as the sun began to pour straight down through the jagged lightning-bolt opening at the top.

"A few things you ought to know, Hawke. First, Carmody probably thinks he heard men and horses massing in the next bowl. I would expect that to happen. Second, take a close look at your friend.

He's trying not to show it, but that bullet went clean through his arm and is lodged in his side. I can see the hole in his shirt and the blood. I don't think it hit lung or guts, but he's losing a lot of blood and I don't think he's going to be much help in a few minutes."

I'd figured as much, so I just nodded and waited for Munro to continue.

"Third, I just checked my timepiece. We've been here for eighteen minutes. And I've just used up thirty seconds running my mouth. I figure there are more hidey-holes here, and more gunmen, maybe good ones this time."

Munro jerked his head toward the end of the pass. "Carmody told us the next bowl is where he saw horses. Think about it: You have men scattered all over the place, you hear gunfire near the front, somebody who escapes says there's a troop of heavily armed men who know what they're doing...what do you do?

"I've thought about it. You gather up your weapons, round up every available man, and plan an attack."

"Which is probably coming any minute."

"Yep."

Munro cut his steel-blue eyes away from the sky for just a second, looked at me, and shrugged.

"And I'm out of ideas, Hawke."

"I'm not," I said.

And then I drew my mount up next to Miller and reached in the saddlebag.

Chapter 37

"I make no guarantees," Miller said as he shook the gray powder from his hands. "This is all eyeball work on my part and we have no idea of the logistics inside."

I nodded and lashed two coal oil lamps on either side of the saddle of the spare horse, making sure the metal rested against the leather. The outsides get hotter than hell and I didn't want to burn the horse. What I didn't know is whether the outside would get hot enough to ignite the leather and wood of the saddle. I doubted it, but what I don't know about fires is considerable, except that I don't like them.

Hoofbeats thudded in the distance. It was Carmody. Moving fast. Not a good sign.

I hated the idea of sacrificing the horse. But it wasn't certain death for the horse. Just probable. Like the situation facing all of us at this moment, it occurred to me.

I nodded to Miller and said, "Proceed."

Miller began lighting the fuses on sticks of explosive he'd trimmed down. Each stick had a percussion cap and maybe an eighth of a stick of explosive left; Miller had dumped the rest and folded the paper tube back. The man knew his business. Whatever his real business was.

He moved to the side of the cave mouth and underhanded the bombs in one-by-one.

The thuds were dull, but we could feel the shock waves come through the mouth and see the light of the explosions and glimpse crazy shadows through the mouth.

I slapped the lantern horse on the croup and yelled *"charge."* Horses can't be trained to recognize words, but they do pick up on things, and "charge" seemed as good a word as any.

He plunged into the unknown, snorting. snarling. If horses could roar, I'm sure he would have.

I came in right behind him with my pistol in hand. The horse looked like a crazy ship in the night, lit up with those lanterns on the side, as it tossed in a violent storm. Somehow, I think he knew his job was to pose a distraction, and he created a wild, insane, haunting one.

As the horse turned crazily, I could see three men and a woman lit up periodically in crazy bright scenes that dissolved into darkness and reappeared again with the people frozen in slightly different positions. It was as though they were standing in front of an insanely spinning lighthouse beacon.

One of the men had been seated at a table and had been knocked to the floor by one of the concussions. He was mesmerized by the display and holding a gun while trying to decide where and what to shoot. He took aim at the spinning horse.

I shot him twice in the head before he could fire.

Then a rifle cracked behind me.

The horse whirled faster.

For a half a second of wild, haunted illumination I saw three people. One was Lydia, still intact after the improvised stun grenades and scowling. The second was a tall man with wide, terrified eyes holding her by the collar of her frilly blue dress and pointing a long revolver at her head. The third was a shorter man who'd dropped his pistol and hugged his chest where Munro's slug had torn into his heart. He'd melted to the ground by the time the light made its next lunatic revolution

"I'll shoot her," the tall one shrilled. He pulled Lydia close and buried his head into the back of her neck and pushed her to the cave opening.

He was smart. He pasted himself up against her and turned her and turned her and turned her again like they were dancing a mad waltz toward the mouth of the cave. Each twirl was caught like some sort of crazy series of ghostly daguerreotypes by the revolving beacon of the spinning horse, who began to snort and whinny and kick, knocking over the table.

The tall one speed-waltzed Lydia into the dim sunshine.

"We're taking a horse," he said. "If I see you follow, she dies."

His gun hand was trembling violently. I was afraid that we'd come all this way with a purpose to save her and she was about to die by accident.

I was outside the mouth and Munro was behind me. Harbold still sighted a line in front of the third cave.

And beyond him was Carmody's horse. It was riderless. I felt a sickness gnaw somewhere deep inside.

"*Hold all fire*," Harbold commanded.

"What?" Munro said.

It didn't make sense to me either. Was he talking to the gunman? Why?

To us? *Why?*

And then the answer arrived from the sky.

Chapter 38

"*Flying friendly incoming,*" Carmody yelled from above, the words still being spoken as his great jumble of long arms and legs avalanched on top of the gunman.

The impact was astonishingly sudden and violent. Carmody weighs, I would guess, upwards of 220 pounds and I have no idea from where he launched himself, but it must have been a high ledge because he hit with an impact that shook the ground.

Carmody managed to strip the gunman off Lydia's back while inflicting minimal damage on her. She was, in any case, a sturdy woman.

Carmody had managed to wrap his right hand around the gunman's wrist, and for the moment the barrel of the weapon was flat on the ground, pointed away from Lydia.

The gunman tried to work his wrist out of Carmody's grasp and looked like he was succeeding.

And then Lydia Davis stomped down. She was wearing a fancy lace-up boot with a buckle – I guess she liked secure garb, the female equivalent of wearing a belt and suspenders – that had a two-inch heel that curved back under to form a small square that no scientist in the world could have improved upon as a hand-mashing tool.

The man screamed. The gun came loose and lay in the dirt.

Carmody tried to grab it but it was beyond the reach of even his long arm and his palm flopped into the dust six inches away.

Lydia picked it up.

The gunman scrambled back on one hand and his heels, the recently mangled hand shielding his face.

There wasn't much he could say.

He tried, *"No!"*

It didn't work. Lydia shot him six times.

"Asshole," she said.

Chapter 39

Carmody dragged himself to his feet and stumbled.

"There's no time to fuck around," he said, and I noticed his chest was heaving. "Probably ten men are gonna be riding through that pass any minute."

Munro led the horse out of the cave and cut the lanterns off. They lay burning dimly next to the empty gun, which still emitted a faint plume of smoke.

"*Up,*" he commanded Lydia, the need to whisper now obsolete. His basso profundo echoed as he heaved her into the saddle. For a man in his 60s and being so lean he demonstrated considerable strength.

"Lydia," Harbold said, "I've spent an entire day watching this cave. Is there anyone in there?"

"I don't know," she thundered in that booming contralto, and despite the fact that I may have had only seconds to live, I couldn't help but think she and Munro could put on a hell of a performance in a German opera.

"If there *is* anybody in there," Lydia said, "they're *assholes*. I'm the only non-criminal in this shithole."

"Well then," Miller said, lighting a fuse on a full stick, "fuck them."

He galloped in front of the mouth and threw the explosive in. Dust and small rocks blew out the cave opening like it was from the mouth of a cannon.

Harbold, bleeding off what I imagine was a considerable tankful of steam brought on by frustration, fired three times into the mouth, blindly.

"Just for the hell of it," Harbold said. "I haven't shot anybody all day."

He looked genuinely aggrieved, like a petulant child. And then he shot once more and headed toward the way we came in.

We all followed.

Chapter 40

Carmody slumped forward and began to slide off his mount. He was unconscious.

"Shit," Munro said, riding alongside and grabbing a handful of his shirt.

I rode up and tried to push Carmody back on. He was more or less centered, slumped against the withers and crest. We could ride three abreast and keep him from falling, but it would slow us down.

"Move out of the way," Lydia said, riding up from behind me.

I don't know why, but I did what she said.

She pulled up alongside and vaulted off her horse and mounted behind Carmody's saddle, straddling the Morgan's croup. Just like that. Like she did it every day.

"Simple rodeo trick," she said. "It's only hard the first time you do it. Kind of like everything else in life."

And she reached over Carmody and grabbed the reins and dug those hand-crunching square heels into the Morgan's flank and bolted to the front of the pack.

"*Full speed*," she shouted.

"*Full speed,*" Munro echoed.

They both kept yelling in unison and I couldn't help but envision them in helmets with horns, wailing out the finale of something by Wagner.

We entered the bowl where we'd had the first gunfight, and then a bullet shrieked by me, and then two. And then I heard the crackle of gunfire. The lag between the buzz and the bang led me to believe they were some distance *behind* us, and not shooting from above. It was a guess, based on the fact that rifle fire usually travels a bit faster than sound. I couldn't locate the source of any sound in the crazy echo chamber, but if they were shooting from perches in the bowl we'd be dead by now.

I fought the temptation to turn around to see what was in back of us. No one else turned around, including Lydia. Looking back slows you down. I don't know why, and I know it doesn't make sense, but it does. You also stand the risk of riding into something you would have seen if looking forward. Looking back also makes you a bigger target. And it *also* makes it more likely you'll get shot in the face instead of the ass, so I made it a point to hunker down and urged the Morgan on.

And then it occurred to me.

"*Shit.* Lydia, take a deep breath and hold it. Everybody, hold your breath."

Lydia shrugged, and, as though she were accustomed to accommodating lunatics, inhaled deeply as we entered the pass.

The noise of the horses in full gallop in the confined walls was like being physically battered.

The riderless horse was in the lead and pulling away. A little less weight makes a big difference in an all-out sprint. And so does more weight: The horse bearing Carmody and Lydia was lagging.

"I'm going to fall behind and hold them off," I shouted, though I wasn't sure if anybody could hear me. And then I forgot and inhaled a lungful of that foul air and started coughing.

"I wouldn't shoot a gun in here," Miller said. "This is *methane*." And then he coughed.

"What the hell is methane?" Lydia sputtered.

"Shut up and *ride*," Munro roared, and we did. Ahead, at the opening of the canyon, there was a glow of sunshine, like a distant star.

I fell back anyway because this time I actually needed to turn around and take a look. When we broke into the sunshine I wouldn't be able to see the pursuers in the darkness and I had to know what we'd be up against.

As near as I could tell in the dim light of the pass, there were a dozen men, all of them wearing bandanas over their mouths. Why that would help you breathe with a gas that robs you of air I didn't know, but it was obvious they'd traveled this route before. Maybe they just wanted to keep the stink out.

I looked forward and saw that Miller was out in the open already. He was light and an excellent rider. He maintained his balance while nonchalantly digging into the saddlebag for the dynamite and matches with both hands.

Munro broke through next, followed by Harbold. They knew what was coming and needed to get a couple hundred yards ahead before turning to fire.

I was only a length behind Carmody and Lydia.

"Keep going," I yelled. "No matter what you see, just *ride right into it.*"

I was momentarily blinded when I broke through.

Then I heard the pounding concussion of the blasts and put my head down and spurred the Morgan.

When my vision cleared, I could see the Apaches.

Chapter 41

Taza and his half-dozen men had done magnificent work.

When our pursuers broke through, they took a look and turned back immediately, their horses bumping and circling as their riders cursed and yelped and bickered.

We opened fire on them, and they panicked.

They retreated back into the opening of the canyon.

Apaches are nomads by custom. They can erect surprisingly comfortable buffalo-skin teepees in a matter of minutes and some can construct domed wickiups in a couple of hours. So moving around some rocks and placing some logs that at a casual glance appear like light artillery emplacements – especially to men who have just emerged from twilight into blinding sunshine and heard blasts of undetermined origin – isn't much of a challenge.

The odds were in our favor now, even without the mocked-up guns. Even if there were a hundred pursuers, we had seven armed Apaches, four experienced gunfighters, enough guns, ammunition and dynamite to start a mining company *and* an army, and perhaps our most formidable weapon: a newly freed woman with revenge on her mind and the apparent ability to exact it.

Moreover, they had to come out in the open to meet us, and we had some cover from which to shoot.

But we also had a wounded man who could die without medical attention. We couldn't wait there forever.

But neither could the outlaws, because they'd suffocate in the gassy passage.

One of the canyon dwellers, a lanky fellow with long, greasy hair, was the last to retreat to the opening. He had a strategy in mind: take a gulp of air, duck back where he couldn't be seen, and fire.

We could see him outlined in the gloom as he brought a rifle to his shoulder.

Miller raised a finger and shouted. "I wouldn't…"

He stopped and looked at me.

"Should I tell them?"

Munro butted in.

"Why the hell should we…"

And then the rifle went off, spitting fire in the gloom, and there was a *whoosh* and the tunnel lit up with a harsh blue light.

Chapter 42

"I don't think that was enough of an explosion to kill anybody," Miller said. "Gave them a pretty good sunburn though, I imagine."

We'd tended to Carmody as best we could. Taza had torn some strips from his tunic and constructed bandages and a sling.

Carmody came to a few times and mumbled something about Mrs. Ulysses S. Grant and then drifted off again. We tied him to his horse and headed for Gray Springs, the nearest town with a doctor. Miller knew the way.

"What *was* that stuff? Harbold asked.

"Gas from swamp," Taza said. "Like swamp farting."

"That's exactly right," Miller said. "It's formed by decomposing matter, and you find that in a swamp and in your guts. Ben Franklin wrote about it. Called it 'flammable air.' I was a mining engineer and it's common, though I never saw a concentration like that."

"It smells like shit," Lydia said.

Miller actually smiled. For the first time I'd seen, ever.

"Methane itself doesn't smell. It's the rotting stuff that produces it that stinks."

"And scares big war hero," Taza said.

Of course, that was directed at me.

"What are you talking about?" I asked. "You're the one who gave me that 'bad medicine' excuse because you were afraid of the place."

"Not afraid. But not stupid, either. Apache is smart enough to not go where air stinks and blows up."

We rode for a while in silence.

"Most Apache, anyway. I get worried and come in to save you, that show I have bigger heart than brain. I saw end of fight. Flying mountain man pretty quick for man his size."

More silence.

"Old man with voice like goose move like young warrior. I read a lot of books written in English and learn word for old man like that, but I forget."

"*Spry*," I said.

Miller looked back at me.

"I don't like that word."

"Neither do I," Munro said.

"Anyway," Taza said, "you all very good fighters. When I saw I did not have to save, how do you say it – *your sorry asses* – I come back to stand by phony guns."

"Thank you," I said.

"You are fine warrior."

"Thank you," I said, and meant it this time.

"It will be honor to kill you someday. But that is after you keep your promise. You remember promise you made to me to get me to do all this? Promise that make me breathe air that smell like back end of buffalo and play with sticks when I should be working?"

I assured him that I did and would take care of it as soon as possible.

No one spoke until we reached Gray Springs.

Chapter 43

The doctor told us that Carmody had lost a lot of blood and had a shattered rib where the bullet had lodged, but barring any infection or other complications he would be back on his feet in a week or two, although the arm could take months to heal.

Carmody was drifting in and out the first night when Munro said he was leaving to take Lydia back to Austin the next day. Harbold would go with them.

Carmody waved weakly and in a creaky voice asked Lydia to say hello to President Grant for him.

"I get a lot of that," she shrugged.

Munro sent a telegram to Judge Gates Davis to let him know that Lydia was safe and unharmed, and at my request he cabled Elmira to let her know that I was safe and Carmody, while injured, would recover, and I would be along in a couple of days.

I asked Miller if there was anyone who should be notified, but he shook me off.

"The kid who cleans up for me has been handling the shop and I told him I had to leave on a family emergency," he said. "Let's leave it at that."

Munro and Lydia slept late the next morning.

They slept late *together*. Harbold spotted them coming out of the same hotel room.

"That is a very strange romance," Harbold told me as Munro and Lydia's thunderous bass voices rumbled a duet as they walked down the street.

"You mean a May-December-kind-of-strange romance?" I asked.

"No, I mean *the-two-scariest-people-in-the-world-somehow-find-each-other* type of romance."

He shook his head for a full minute.

There would be some housekeeping to take care of over the next few days and weeks. Munro needed the horses back, so I'd have to ride to Austin with my own horse and the cavalry mounts and return home.

We'd also have to sort out whether we wanted to return to the Canyon of the Long Shadows and finish up the job. It appeared there was substantial reward money to be collected, and when Carmody and I perused some more wanted posters, we thought we might find a few more golden eggs in that basket of thieves and killers.

Also, justice seemed to dictate that we go back and clean up the mess. But I was in no hurry; each experience with white-hot flying lead trying to embed itself in my brain increases my appreciation of being alive and bolsters my determination to stay that way.

Then, there was the problem of Gillis and Weed. Munro had said that Davis had promised to make the problem go away but wasn't too clear on the precise mechanism.

I didn't worry about it until two days later. I'd stayed by Carmody's bedside as he regained his senses, what senses he possessed, anyway, and slept in the chair beside his bed as he moaned an accompaniment to his nightmares about, from what I could understand of his mumblings, exploding farts and the president's wife.

I took walks, ate a lot, and on a whim stopped by the local bank to have a talk about the evils of paper currency in general and Greenbacks in specific.

I left early on Friday. Miller would stay another couple days and travel back to Shadow Valley with Carmody when the doctor said it was safe.

I took my time getting back. I was anxious to see Elmira and sleep in my own bed – her bed, actually – but I enjoyed the traveling, too. There's some beautiful country to the northwest of my adopted home.

I'm not an outdoorsman like Carmody. I have a complicated relationship with nature: I appreciate its beauty but at the same time am no fan of bugs, snakes, heat, cold, and the exquisite variety of nature's booby traps – vines, chuckholes, and the like – designed by some higher power to make you fall down and hurt important and painful parts of your body.

It was about an hour from sunset when I got off the trail near the delta and headed into town. It was quiet for a Friday night.

I wanted a beer, a bath, and a bed, in that order.

The Spoon seemed subdued.

And so, oddly, did Elmira.

She smiled, but it was tentative. And when I kissed her, she kissed back but it was short and perfunctory.

I asked her what was wrong. She said nothing was wrong; she was just unnerved by the danger I'd faced and the fact that Carmody had been injured.

But she told me I had done a good thing, even though she seemed inexplicably uncertain about it.

And she also told me that Judge Gates Davis was here, in her back office, to thank me personally.

That was nice, I supposed. A beer would have been better, but that could wait. I was bone-tired as I followed her in to meet the judge and get it over with.

Judge Davis was seated at her desk with his fingers interlaced and an expression that said he was waiting a second to make up his mind about me. He raised a hand and beckoned for me to come forward, wagging all four fingers, and then made a palm-up gesture toward the chair he wanted me to occupy.

I sat down.

From behind me I heard the unmistakable sound of a rifle cocking, and an oily voice told me to raise my hands.

I did, and a hand slithering in from behind snatched my revolver out of the holster.

Then Jefferson Gillis came through the door and sat on the edge of the desk.

He smiled at me.

Chapter 44

People who've never been knocked unconscious don't understand the process.

You hardly ever remember the blow that put you out. Sometimes, you might not remember anything for the minute before having your lights turned off, or the hour, or even the whole day. If you've lost a lot of memory, some part of it usually comes back to you, but never the moment of the blow.

When I woke up in the cot in my own cell, I didn't remember what happened but was able to put two and two together. There was a long and painful bruise on the back of my head and a cut at the top of the crease. The bruise, I surmised, came from a gun barrel and the cut from the sight digging into my scalp as the barrel slid across. When I felt the wound, my hand came away covered with brown, clotted blood.

It takes about an hour for blood to turn that color.

I sat upright and the room began to spin, so I lay back and turned on my side to get an idea of what was going on.

A kid with a droopy lower lip and dull dark eyes was sitting at my desk. Wordlessly, without changing expression, he arose and walked out of the room, not bothering to shut the door.

I was able to stand up by the time he reappeared with Gillis, Davis, and two other men.

Droopy and the strangers were obviously hired muscle.

Droopy didn't worry me too much, nor did the oaf who entered after him. He was a doughy man with a two-day growth of beard and a paunch and a body odor that could etch glass. Stinky looked dirty; even the whites of his eyes looked like they needed a cleaning. I pegged him and Droopy as exemplars of the species of losers who realized they couldn't handle the tedium and labor of a cattle drive and now postured as tough guys while scraping for a few dollars here and there, working in the margins of the outlaw world.

But there was one other man. He looked like the real article.

I recognized him.

In those dime novels you read about lawmen who scour their wanted posters and through preposterous coincidence just happen to bump into the perpetrator next week.

That sort of coincidence never happens. Until it does.

Droopy and Stinky instinctively edged aside as Ben Tremaine stepped between them.

Chapter 45

There'd probably never been that big a crowd in my office before.

Judge Gates Davis, who seems to like other people's desks, took a seat at mine, though he had to turn his chair 90 degrees to face me. It wasn't easy for him; he probably weighed 280 pounds.

Gillis, who seemed to like leaning on desks, rested the considerable mass of his hip on the corner, with portions of it dangling below the edge. It looked uncomfortable digging into him like that, but he apparently liked the posture.

Percival Weed stood in the corner, shifting his weight from foot to foot and blinking a lot. He'd taken off the robe and wore a suit that had probably looked pretty sharp a week ago. Now it had turned into rumpled leaves of black cabbage.

Droopy and Stinky stood on either side of the room and Tremaine planted himself behind Judge Davis.

I heard the wail coming toward us. It grew in volume, an unceasing howl of despair, until it hovered outside the door.

The door opened and Elmira walked in, wailing some more.

She lunged toward the cell door and nobody stopped her, and then she realized there wasn't much she could do when she got there, so she leaned her head against the bars and decided to keep wailing.

"I didn't want to," she said, and then tried to catch her breath. Wailing takes it out of a person.

Gillis heaved himself off the edge of my desk and grabbed her by the shoulder.

"Get out," he said, and gave her a shove toward the door.

"I *believed* you," Elmira said to Gillis, and panted for a moment.

Gillis ignored her, so she turned to me.

"He told me he cared, and I believed him."

I leaned my arms against the bars and looked at the floor. I wasn't angry. Not at her, anyway. At least not too angry at her.

"Those words," I said, "have caused more misery throughout history than almost anything else every spoken. 'He told me he cared.' How could you fall for that? That's the second-biggest lie in history."

Elmira took a deep breath and told me what I knew was coming.

"He said what he was doing was *for your own good.*"

"And that's the first-biggest lie in history."

Elmira pulled herself up to the bars and began whispering, as though the crew five feet away somehow wouldn't be able to hear.

"Mr. Gillis said you had to be arrested. And he said that if they did it the normal way, you might fight back and you'd be killed. So I made sure nothing happened. They promised that you'd be all right and that the system would be fair."

I looked straight at her and her face twisted back into a mask of misery and she let loose with a cry of primal anguish. I actually felt badly for her. She was no kid and no dummy. She'd survived in a tough world and a tougher business and shown more than her share of resilience and smarts.

And she was not the first woman or man to fall victim to a smooth talker who says one thing and does another. In her case, it was a politician with a broad Southern accent who assured her that *"ahhh care 'bout you,"* but wasn't above shoving her around a bit.

Which he did, again. Gillis grabbed a handful of her dress and pushed her hard against the bars.

"Shut up," he said.

There are plenty more of his type. The society lady who raises money for charity and gets her name in the paper for her effort but fires the maid for missing a morsel of dirt on the floor. The big people of the world who loudly proclaim their support for the little people of the world but wouldn't be caught dead actually interacting with one of them, except maybe to hire one to shine their shoes.

Elmira was gullible. But honest.

There were only two other honest people in the room.

I like to think I was one of them. Tremaine was the other. We were both in the business of killing and knew it and admitted it and didn't tell anyone it was for their own good.

Tremaine wanted me dead after he'd tortured some information out of me, and he wanted to be paid well at the end of the deal, and that's the straightforward reason why he was here.

I wanted Tremaine dead because I wanted to stay alive, but also because I wanted to *win,* and I also wanted the rest of them dead – if it became convenient and I could get away with it – because I hated them and their kind.

Tremaine was following my thoughts, or maybe it just seemed that way, because he nodded.

He pulled Gillis's hand from Elmira and slowly turned her toward the door, marching her out at a methodical and measured pace.

When he shut the door behind her, he turned and told me that things didn't look too good for me.

Chapter 46

"The kid died," Davis said.

I knew he expected me to ask *what kid,* but I didn't want to let him get too comfortable. You play a man's game by his rules and he generally thinks straight. I needed to throw him off-track.

"The kid died," Davis said again, tapping an index finger on my desk. "The one you beat so badly when Gillis came to talk with you. He died a couple days later of his injuries."

"You mean Bucktooth," I said. "I doubt that he's dead, and if he is, *you* killed him."

I was going to mention that it was really Carmody who scrambled the kid's eggs but didn't want to seem like I was passing the buck.

"It was you," Davis said. "He came to see you and you instigated violence and he wound up dead. You're just as guilty no matter who did what. That's murder."

Percival Weed cleared his throat and looked uneasy.

"Sir, I'm sure you meant to add that a murder charge is not always the case when –"

Davis cut him off as though he hadn't heard.

"And as I am a *real* judge, as you like to say, I can hold court right here."

Gillis settled himself back on the corner of the desk.

"And as a member of the governing body of this town," Gillis said, "I can appoint Tremaine as marshal and he can see that the legally determined sentence is carried out."

Weed cleared his throat again and Davis silenced him with a glare.

Davis leaned back in my chair and touched the fingertips of both hands in front of his chest. He was a big man, fat but broad-shouldered, with longish dark hair and an expression that betrayed the self-assured zeal of a fire-and-brimstone preacher. He carried himself in a way that was reminiscent of eras gone by, both in his mannerisms and his dress.

"That sentence, my friend, is largely something you'll determine for yourself. Let's walk very carefully through the next couple minutes here and see how much help you can be."

Weed reached into a briefcase.

"Do you need a gavel, Sir?"

Davis looked at the ceiling for a minute and was about to speak again when I cut in.

"You're going to tell me you'll make this go away if I tell you where the ransom money is. I assume you've already strong-armed the bank manager and he's showed you his cupboards are bare."

"All right," Davis said, drawing out the words and ending on a high note so I knew it was a question.

"But I want something in return," I said. "It's no skin off your back. We both know you're going to kill me anyway. I just want to know why you're doing this."

The judge's face was flinty and his eyes focused a hundred feet in back of me. He probably practiced that look, along with the old-fashioned mannerisms.

"That's assuming you know why you're doing this," I said. "Maybe you don't. Maybe you're just acting on orders. You're probably not high enough in the food chain to know the whole story. Or that you're afraid to tell it to me."

I knew that what I'd said was not true, but I wanted to goad him.

A lot of men can train themselves to hide their expressions, but some just can't stop whatever mechanism it is that sends blood rushing to their faces. His cheekbones and forehead were crimson.

I *had* him. He couldn't help but set me straight.

"What is it you're incapable of understanding?" he asked.

"Why the staged kidnapping? Why the ambush? What's so important about killing me?"

"You got *in my way*," Davis said, and it was a growl of barely restrained fury.

"In the way of *what?* A year ago, I broke up a scheme to drive Elmira out of her business and sell it to a stooge. I assume you were behind that?"

He said nothing, but his face was mottled now, with blotches around his eyes like the mask of a red-faced raccoon.

"I get that part," I said. "You found out that there was a railroad going through her property and there was a lot of money to be made if you acquired property along the route before anybody knew, while it was just scrub wilderness. The developers would come running to you with money in hand after the route was announced, or maybe you'd build it up yourself with hotels and casinos and the like. Either way, you'd make a fortune."

He said nothing, so I continued.

"But you couldn't very well be seen profiting directly from secret information, so you flooded the town with muscle and drove Elmira's customers away, and your thugs took over the only other bar in town and tried to force her to sell to the owner, who was under your thumb. An amazing plan."

Except for the blushing predilection – which was almost like a dial that I could read the same way a train engineer detects how hot the boiler is – Davis could hold a good poker face.

But I noticed his eyes widened a little when I praised his cunning.

So now I knew what to do, and it was time to move in.

"And that was *brilliant*," I said. "I'll give you that."

I actually wasn't lying about that part.

Davis liked what I said. He actually nodded a little.

"But there's still something that I just will never be able to understand. I just can't scheme like you, I guess. You totally lost me."

Davis lifted an eyebrow and prepared to hold forth, like a professor about to explain a concept to a slow student, prepared to bask in his superiority.

"What exactly don't you understand?"

"What the hell is so important about the land where the railroad is going? I understand that there's a lot of money to be made, and the first attempt might have been worth it. But round two … staging the kidnapping of *your own daughter* to lure me into an ambush. Hiring Tremaine?"

I wasn't acting now; I really wanted fill in the blanks. The fact that he staged the kidnapping was just a guess, but he didn't correct me.

So I'd guessed right.

"All that money," I said, "and all that risk. Setting up Gillis here as some sort of shadow government. Making Weed come down here and try to hand down bogus rulings. Attempted murder of a marshal. What in God's name is back there? Gold? Silver? Carmody and I have been over and over that patch of scrub and we can't find anything. What could possibly be back there that's worth all this?"

Davis leaned forward and almost whispered.

"It's what *will* be there. *Your dead body.*"

He pounded his fist on my desk three times. Steady beats like a machine, each one harder than the one before. He was shaking with fury.

"You're going to die because you fucked up my deal and made me *look bad.* In front of *my colleagues.*"

In front of his *colleagues.* His *colleagues.*

I almost laughed, but it was more sad than funny, and I actually felt my shoulders slump. Word choices lead us to interesting and scary crevices of the human mind, and here they had just provided an unintentionally trenchant insight into Davis's world.

His colleagues are what I'd call accomplices.

I shook my head, trying to clear it, so I could think clearly when I started the fight for my life.

I made up my mind how to start.

Chapter 47

"I'll make you a deal," I said.

Gillis snorted and laughed at me. Davis said nothing

"Davis," I said, "I'll use my connections to get them to go easy on you."

The audacity of it caught him off guard.

Gillis make that snorting sound again, and Droopy and Stinky looked amused, glancing back at each other several times, poking each other, as though it were a long-practiced ritual. I surmised that they were easily amused.

Weed looked thoughtful and troubled.

Tremaine had no reaction. He just watched me. Just looked. He made no attempt to glare or posture or to look tough, and the fact that he didn't feel the need to try worried me.

I turned my attention to Gillis.

"But you, you're on your own. You're an even lower species that Davis here. He's just a crook. You're a *parasite.* You find vulnerable people who believe your bullshit and you suck the life out of them."

Gillis, of course, had an innate need to act tough, because he wasn't. He sauntered up to the bars, though not quite close enough for me to reach him. He sneered at me.

"As for you two," I said to Droopy and Stinky, "you're too stupid to know any better. Leave now and I'll forget I saw you."

Stinky gave a wheezy laugh that started and ended abruptly, like a cat hissing.

I returned my attention to Davis.

"I know what's on your mind, Davis. You want the money back. Though not in the way a normal man wants money. You want it back because each of those bills has your arrest warrant written on it."

Droopy and Stinky were still poking each other and Gillis was still sneering but I had Weed's attention.

And Davis's.

"I buried that money, but not before I gave a bill each to Munro, Harbold, and Carmody," I lied. It would have been an excellent idea, but I hadn't thought of it until now. I reminded myself to start thinking more clearly about the future, if indeed it turned out I would have one.

But they didn't know I lied.

"I told them to hang onto it and to take it to Washington if anything happened to me. Don't worry, Davis, I replaced each greenback with my own money. Didn't want to be caught stealing in front of my *colleagues*."

Davis surely could run a range of colors like a chameleon. He was a pale gray now.

"I knew there was something fishy about that money. On the back it said, 'tens note is legal tender.' I guess that could be the right way to word something on a ten-dollar Greenback, which is all I had, but it's a pretty convoluted way to put it. So when I was waiting for Carmody to heal up, I checked with the local banker and he told me that there was a huge run of counterfeits with that error."

I figured I might as well take my last shot, and I gave Davis my best hard-case stare and continued.

"So the way I see it, Davis, ten grand of these Greenbacks were sitting around in an evidence vault for some counterfeiting trial and you 'borrowed' them for the payoff. You'd have easy access. All you had to do is say you wanted to examine some evidence. It's a hell of a lot easier than stealing actual cash, or God forbid, using your own money. And there was no risk. Your henchmen would kill me on the way out of town, when I didn't expect an ambush, and retrieve it.'"

Now Davis was on his feet, thinking, plotting, moving toward me. His face was red again. His lecture wasn't working out as planned.

I began to yell.

"You're *through,* Davis. You can kill me, but Carmody knows about the counterfeits, Harbold knows, and most important, Munro knows. You're going to kill us all? You think *I'm* a pain in the ass? Wait until you get *Munro* on your case. And he's a state senator. You think you can kill him with a bunch of sad-sack hired goons?"

"I'm fully capable of dealing with them one at a time," Davis said, taking a step closer to the bars and standing with his legs spread and his hands on his hips.

"I do one thing, finish it, and then move on," Davis said. "Right now, unfortunately for you, you are the complete focus of my attention."

"Davis, there's one more thing. Your daughter is no dummy. She's going to figure out you used her. Why would you do something like that?"

And then the answer hit me. I'd only been taunting him, and didn't have the answer to the question, but now I'd figured it out.

Sometimes your mind works best when you're cornered – as I now *literally* was, trapped in an eight-by-twelve corner cell surrounded by six men who had everything to lose if I lived.

Chapter 48

"I'll give the devil his due, Davis," I said. "It was a fucking *incredible* scheme. I just figured the whole thing out."

"You think so? Tell me."

Davis put a hand on his hip and lifted his eyebrows to let me know he was waiting. His face remained set in the serious stony countenance that people of his strata employ to pose for historical commemoration. He looked for all the world like a statue from a bygone era, what with his double-breasted tailed coat, two-toned lapels, and wing collar over the type of neck sash that Daniel Webster wore in the 1840s.

"Tell me." The eyes turned harder.

I held up my index finger.

"First, using your daughter as a pawn in the game completely insulated you from suspicion, didn't it? You're at the center of this web, but you wove the strands in such an overlapping and tangled pattern that no one could follow it back to you."

I lifted another finger, a habit Carmody occasionally mimicked, and when he'd had a few drinks and wanted to parody my long-windedness he'd theatrically take off his shoes. It always got a laugh from his ashram at the bar. He was a natural entertainer, but sometimes I wondered about the wisdom of my carrying a gun in his presence.

But fuck it, I thought, this was complicated, and I was figuring out the details as I went, so I'd unravel the story it my own way.

"Second," I said, holding up the appropriate finger, "you sent Weed on a fool's errand to start some trouble, piss me off, and get myself into a jam."

Weed was a study in slow, horrified realization. His eyes and his mouth and even his nostrils grew wider as it sunk in. He glanced between me and Davis as if looking for an answer.

I popped up my ring finger next.

"Third, you used a crew of henchmen to stage the kidnapping of your daughter, conveniently leaving a survivor – an innocent man, totally uninvolved in the whole affair – to communicate the ransom plan."

Gates nodded and there was a flicker of upward movement at the corners of his mouth. He was particularly proud of that part, I imagined, but men like him rarely smile broadly, finding it undignified.

"Fourth, you fooled a neutral party I trusted – Munro – into asking me to deliver the ransom. In exchange, you offered to get me off the hook for throwing Weed in jail. Separate strands, and again, they appear totally unconnected."

I almost slapped my forehead but didn't want to give them the pleasure.

Then it occurred to me that the more I kept Davis pleased with himself, self-absorbed, and marinating in self-congratulation, the better the chances were for my survival.

So I slapped my forehead.

"Then it was *simple,* I said. "Everybody figured I'd be on guard when I approached Table Top, but you and your men figured I'd be easy pickings when I was still hours away, distracted because I was trying to wind through a wooded trail, and traveling light because I had to keep a low profile. And who would be surprised when a man carrying a lot of money was murdered and robbed on the trail?"

I restrained myself from holding up my thumb to accentuate the fifth and last point, as that's an ungainly gesture, so I folded my arms across my chest. I stepped back and leaned against the wall to the right of the cot.

I looked down and whispered in what I hoped was a convincing tone of bitterness and despair.

"Goddamnit, Davis, you covered all the angles. Even if someone were suspicious after my death, who would follow up? Gillis here would put himself in power and no one connected to Shadow Valley would be able to follow up even if they wanted to."

I slumped a little more, feeling the scratch of the bricks against my shoulder blades, and spoke to the floor in a whisper that was barely audible even to me.

"And you know what the best part was?" I whispered.

Davis, irritated, turned what I would take to be his better ear toward me and took a step forward so he could glory in hearing about the best part.

"If Carmody survived the ambush, he wouldn't be a deputy any longer, anyway. Elmira would be on the outs, too."

I lowered my voice as much as you can while still making a sound.

"Judge Davis," I whispered, "you've gotten your revenge. And you played me like Paganini played the violin."

I liked the Paganini analogy. I'd never seem Paganini play, of course. He died when I was ten or so and as far as I know never traveled to America, but I'd studied a little about him and liked how he went about things.

A violin has four strings tuned to different pitches. You can play chords by playing two more strings together when drawing the bow over them, and you can play individual notes. If one of the strings breaks, you can, in theory at least, calculate what the note would be if played on another string and play using whatever strings are left.

Paganini was perhaps the greatest virtuoso who ever lived, according to what I'd read, and would *intentionally* play with frayed strings, hoping that one would break and he could dazzle the audience by finishing the piece on three strings.

He liked the risk. And he liked the thrill of playing on three strings.

I like it, too.

I'm not that tall, a little over six feet, but I have long arms and broad shoulders and big hands – an ideal build for a fighter, I've been told.

I held up my right hand and wiped my face from forehead to chin and shook my head in exhaustion, keeping my hand over my mouth and rubbing my chin and I wept my words into my oversized palm.

"And there's one more thing."

Even when a fighter gets his brains scrambled, which mercifully I had not, he almost always retains his sense of distance. By that I mean he can gauge to a fraction of an inch whether his fist will reach his opponent's chin or gut.

"One more thing," I whispered.

Davis leaned in by a half inch and I sprang forward and seized one of his fancy velvet lapels up high, near his neck. It was excellent fabric, feeling in my hand to be as strong as tent canvas, and it held firm when I wrenched him forward.

His head hit the bars with such force that I could see flakes of rust and dust begin to snow down on us. Davis's face, which one could charitably call fleshy, was now squeezed between the bars. His lips, nose, and ample cheeks were oozing through a bit, and I was able to slap the protruding parts with considerable vigor.

I put my face right up against his, our noses touching.

"Just so you know," I said, "your daughter, who you were willing to sacrifice in a pawn's gambit so you could kill me, wasn't fooled. She told me you're an asshole."

And then I spit on him.

Chapter 49

Davis bucked in a rage. He was a big man, and when he struck the bars it looked and sounded like a bull going berserk in a rodeo chute.

I twisted Davis's nose and he let out an enraged grunt.

Droopy and Stinky had stopped poking each other and watched the scene in slack-jawed wonder.

Tremaine's hand moved reflexively toward his gun, but hovered an inch above the butt. He couldn't kill me; not yet. Not until I'd told them where the money was hidden. And besides, his boss was between me and his bullets, and slaughtering your cash cow is bad for business.

Gillis pulled the keyring off the nail on the opposite wall, handed it to Stinky, and shoved him toward the door.

In order for this to work, I knew, somebody had to open that door fast.

Stinky, of course, fumbled with the keys. There were only three keys on the ring. Two were small and I still had no idea what they were for. One was large, and presumably most of the higher life forms on the planet could deduce that it was the key to the cell door, but Stinky pondered as though he were solving an equation in celestial mechanics.

Gillis seized the ring and fumbled with the lock himself.

I'd twisted Davis's nose about as far as it would turn, so I went to work on his ear. Davis stuck both arms through the bars but he had no leverage and could only pat my shoulders as he flailed at me.

He screamed and tried to pull away, but that made it hurt more.

Stinky and Droopy poured through the open door.

I ignored them and concentrated on twisting Davis's earlobe.

Stinky grabbed my arms from behind and I played along and allowed him to pull my elbows behind me.

Droopy went to work on my stomach. I let him have a couple of shots and pretended they hurt.

"No," Tremaine said. "Let me handle this."

Davis spoke through clenched teeth.

"You'll do what I tell you when I tell you."

Davis wiped the stream of blood from under his nose and shoved Droopy aside.

He wanted me for himself.

He wanted to beat the location of the money out of me, which promised to be a long ordeal considering I actually didn't know where Carmody had hidden it, and then he wanted me to die, but not too quickly.

But first he just wanted to beat me for the fun of it.

Stinky locked his arms more tightly around my elbows, drawing my shoulders back.

Droopy was reduced to the status of a confused spectator. His hand hovered near his gun, too, but he was unsure of what to do.

There were two other exposed guns in the room. Stinky wore one, very low on his thigh, in the style of men who have never been in a gunfight but who like people to think that they have.

Tremaine wore his with the butt at wrist level in a utilitarian holster. Tremaine looked worried now. Presumably, his payoff depended on keeping me alive until I coughed up the money. He had a job to do and now his boss was in the way. Literally, because Davis's bulk was between me and Tremaine.

Davis snarled. His lips drew back and his face twisted into a mask of hatred as he let out a scream of rage that came from the ground up.

He drew back a meaty, square fist.

I was hoping he'd go for my gut first, and he obliged.

It hurt, but I twisted with it and deflected some of the impact, and more importantly I had an excuse to double over.

I forced myself to wait. In order for this work, it had to unfold all at once, and I had to strike at the last, the very last, the *exquisitely* last moment.

Chapter 50

Stinky started pulling me back so my head would come up and Davis could work on my gut some more.

I sprang up as hard as I could and flung my head back. Stinky was a tall man, which was convenient because the back of my head hit him square on the nose. I could feel it crush and hear the snap.

Stinky screamed and I felt his hands go to his face, and then I reached back and drew *his* gun.

He wore it too low, but with his height it was at a perfect spot for me; all I had to do was move my hand back an extra few inches and there it was.

It was a nice gun, too. It melted right into my hand and slid out of the holster so quickly that I could hear the hiss of metal on leather.

Of course it felt nice. I realized that it was *mine*. The aromatic fucker had stolen it after I'd been knocked out in Elmira's office.

It was a beautiful gun, particularly right now, as it was pointed directly at Gates's forehead.

To my left, Droopy began to move.

He'd made the decision to draw but thought about it too long, so I had time to slice the edge of my hand across his throat. His eyes bulged in eloquent panic as he clawed at his crushed airway.

I grabbed Davis by the hair and spun him around. When you have control of the head, the body generally follows and I was able to edge out of the cell, bulldogging Davis along and keeping him as a shield between me and Tremaine.

For the moment, I had the extra ace.

Tremaine was in the employ of Davis, and thus had nothing to gain and everything to lose by killing him.

I, on the other hand, had a remote interest in keeping Davis alive for his utility as a human shield, but if he were killed I'd not shed a tear and in fact wouldn't really be much worse off. It would be me and Tremaine, pretty much the way things stood with Gates alive, and now I had a gun.

Tremaine had no option, at least for the moment.

Without taking his eyes off me, Tremaine used his left hand to flip my desk up on its end, demonstrating considerable strength. It was solid oak and heavy, as I'd learned when I'd dragged it closer to the window so I could get a little more daylight.

The desk rocked a couple of times and then settled; it looked bigger from this orientation, standing almost six feet tall now.

Tremaine took cover behind it.

I gave a yank to Gates's hair and he half-stumbled, moving another pace toward the door.

Gates held a hand out toward the desk.

"Help me."

Tremaine had a decision to make, and fast. So did I.

Stinky and Droopy were out of commission. Droopy was possibly out of the game for good; I'd connected pretty solidly with his larynx.

Gillis and Weed were, for the moment, frozen in terror to the right of the door. They weren't openly carrying but could be concealing.

Tremaine was behind the desk, and like me, he'd have to do something soon.

His problem was that I was hiding behind the considerable bulk of Judge Gates Davis. Even a professional like Tremaine could not expect to emerge from behind the desk, shoot me in an inadvertently exposed part of my body, and somehow rescue Davis. Even if Tremaine somehow managed to make his bullets curve around Davis and shoot me in the head, I'd mostly likely kill Davis by pulling the trigger in my death reflex.

But my problem was that I couldn't hold this position forever, wearing Davis like a blubbery suit of armor. Suppose I managed to work my way out to the street, what then? I had no idea if Davis had other goons in town, and in any event with Tremaine stalking me I'd be dead the minute I left to run for cover or mount a horse.

I could try to shoot through the desk. It was very heavy oak, but I don't think the top would stop a bullet, though it might slow or deflect it to the point where it wouldn't do fatal damage. But there were drawers full of papers and other things, and multiple layers of even thin material can slow or stop a bullet.

So maybe a shot through the center, where there was only one drawer above the kneehole of the upended desk, would penetrate, but it was a gamble.

But if I opened up, Tremaine knew he was likely to be killed if he didn't fire back, so he would shoot regardless of whether Davis was cut down in the crossfire.

Or Tremaine might just say to hell with it right now and drill both of us and ride out of this godforsaken town that seems to draw trouble like a dead horse draws buzzards.

There have been times when I'd had the same thought cross my mind.

Now, just to further complicate matters, Gillis started moving. I risked a flash glance and saw that he was slowly brushing back his jacket, his palm out. The damn fool probably had a gun stuck in his waistband in the hollow of his back.

I'd have to shoot Gillis in the head soon, but that would mean taking my attention away from Tremaine. Shooting him would require a 90-degree pivot.

Weed ... well, he was a wild card. He didn't strike me as the gun-toting type, not in the Gillis mode, anyway. I doubt if Gillis had ever fired a shot in anger, but I'm sure he liked impressing the doves when he undressed and made a show of leaving his iron on the nightstand.

But now Weed was making a move. I heard the rustle of clothing before I saw him break for his briefcase.

I pulled Davis up to me nice and tight, pressing my left side against him so I wouldn't have to pivot as far when I shot Gillis or Weed or both.

And then Weed came up with something in his right hand.

Chapter 51

The purpose of training is to keep you from having to waste time thinking. In my business, if you think too long you're likely to wind up with wings and a harp, so everything has to be automatic.

I'd never been to the Academy, but Munro had, and he was an absolute evangelist about avoiding distraction. He once disciplined my entire platoon, four squads of ten men each, during training because a rifleman had swatted a mosquito from the back of his neck. That moment of sudden movement and inattention, Munro had bellowed, not only could give away a sniper's position but was also one less instant when the rifleman's attention was focused on the enemy.

If was four in the afternoon, and the squad had been training for about an hour. There was no action nearby, and everyone was looking forward to dinner and a night's rest.

Munro made all twelve men in the squad look for the mosquito, telling us we couldn't break until we found it.

After all, he said, that mosquito was *clearly* the most important thing *in the world to us*. After all, one of us had taken his attention off the enemy – armed men sworn to kill us – to swat it.

We never found the bug and didn't get to break until after midnight.

I can't say for sure if all of the platoon lived through the war because we kind of came and went, but I know that I most improbably lived to middle age by never again letting my attention wander during battle.

So had I not been trained in combat, I most certainly would have lost my concentration and asked Judge Percival Weed why he was holding a gavel.

Chapter 52

Weed held the gavel in both hands and rained down blows on Gillis's head.

It wasn't a very big gavel and Weed wasn't very strong, but the device made an impressive *klop* on Gillis's skull after his hat was knocked off and he covered up and sunk to the ground.

"You son of a *bitch,*" Weed said, hammering away at Gillis's hands and head. "You told me this was all sort of legal. That I was helping stop a crooked scheme by that woman who owns the whorehouse."

He brought the gavel down again.

"You said that the marshal was a crook."

Klop.

"You said that hat this would help my career. And now I'm involved in kidnapping and counterfeiting."

Klop klop klop.

"And you…"

Weed was about to move in on Davis when Tremaine took advantage of the commotion and vaulted out the door.

The man moved like the ghost of a mountain lion. He just *disappeared.*

Davis roared.

"You can't run away like this, you fucking piece of chicken liver. I hired you to protect me from him…"

I laid the barrel of my gun across Davis's temple and he stopped talking and toppled like a tree.

But Davis had a durable skull. Hard as I'd clocked him, he still managed to raise himself up on an elbow.

I let Weed finish off the job with his little gavel.

Chapter 53

After I latched the inside shutters on the window and dimmed the lantern, I packed the whole sorry bunch of them, except for Weed, into the cell.

I removed the cell key from the ring and put it in my pocket. In the spirit of pure meanness I left the ring on the floor within arm's reach so whichever of them came to first could occupy themselves with some fruitless frustration.

For someone who had just spent five minutes flailing with a gavel, Weed seemed remarkably composed. He wasn't even breathing hard. What he lacked in strength he seemed to make up for endurance.

"I can't believe he got scared like that and ran," Weed said. "He was supposed to be this fearsome gunfighter."

"He wasn't scared and from what I know he's nobody to mess with. He ran because he could think fast. He knew had no way to win that hand. No way that wouldn't involve killing the man who hired him. I gather there's a big payday for Tremaine when the curtain goes down on this, and if Davis is dead, so is the payday. He's out there, he may have friends, and he's still gunning for me. My problems are just beginning."

"*Our* problems," Weed said. "I'm no longer Gates's lackey. Nor do I want to be. I'm a lawyer and sort of a judge and a damn good one, and I'm probably going to wind up getting disbarred and going to prison. If I wind up getting shot it won't be the worst thing in the world from where I'm standing now."

I heard a moan from somewhere in the pile of bodies in the cell and noted that Davis was starting to come to. Gillis was in a seated position on the cot, back against the wall and chin on chest, and his eyes were fluttering. Stinky lay curled up on the floor clutching his face and Droopy had not yet moved.

"Let's hope it doesn't come to that. Can you shoot?"

Weed picked up the .41 that I'd taken off Gillis. It was a nasty little five-shot model with no trigger guard called a Swamp Angel, the same name given to some rifles and cannons for reasons that have always eluded me.

"I never have," he said, waving the gun in vague directions that included the proximity of my head, "but the process seems straightforward."

I wrapped my fingers around the cylinder to keep the mechanism from moving and gently pulled the gun from his hand.

"This probably isn't the time to learn," I said.

Whatever I was going to do needed to be done soon.

I heard some more stirring behind me and lowered my voice. Unless I killed them all right now, which was an unethical but admittedly alluring option, the events of the next few hours could conspire to put them back in touch with the people who would be hunting me.

"How many other men does Tremaine have?"

"Only one other that I've seen. Not gun-fighter-looking. Scruffy, like the two in there. He's older, maybe in his 50s. Big white beard. Wheezes when he talks. But yesterday I heard Davis talk about getting more men from the canyon to ride here. I don't know if he went through with that, but I did hear him say that those Canyon creatures are very angry at you. Something about setting them on fire?"

I ignored his question and thought about where we stood. Tremaine and Wheezy and any other allies we didn't know about may lay siege to the place at any moment, and if Tremaine just ran out of patience he might start firing blindly through the shuttered windows, on the theory that he was bound to hit something. And there could be a contingent of outlaws with sunburns and a grudge arriving at any time.

I remembered his considerable energy during the gavel attack, and on a hunch I asked him, "Can you run?"

"Like a deer. I ran all sorts of races in school, especially long ones. I wasn't much for team sports."

Somehow that didn't surprise me, but it didn't seem the time to pursue it.

"What I'm going to ask you to do involves considerable risk," I said. "But I'm talking like a lawyer. In plain language, it's likely you're going to get killed. But if we wait here, getting killed is a certainty."

He actually jumped up and down, like a kid who's been chosen for a team for the first time in his life.

"I can do it."

I opened the bottom drawer of the upended desk and pulled out one of the spare round-brimmed hats I favored. I would have given him the ratty one I'd worn after I lost my Boss of the Plains, but that was knocked off my head back in Elmira's office.

"This will give you good luck," I said. I'm not a superstitious man, not exactly, but I'd kept this relic even though it had not one, but *two* bullet holes and had been trampled by a horse. As I'd emerged unscathed from both incidents, I allowed myself to speculate there may have been some supernatural powers connected with it. It was worth keeping, but not wearing. A man has to have some pride in his appearance.

I gave him a holster that, when adjusted to the first belt-hole, barely stayed up. Against my better judgment I let him keep a revolver, the one that I remembered to retrieve from Droopy, and I left it loaded.

"Your mission," I said, noting how he puffed up when hearing the word, "is to draw fire and attention away from me. When we go out, run left, and run like hell. Cut in back of the buildings and keep dodging and ducking. And then get to your horse if you can. If not, steal one. And then ride to Austin and tell Munro or Harbold the story and tell them to get here yesterday."

I wrote down both addresses, moving over to write by the light of lamp on the cabinet, and it occurred to me that I had no idea how long I'd been unconscious and knew only that it had been dark when I woke up. My timepiece was missing and probably in the possession of Stinky or Droopy, but I'd only patted them down for guns.

"Do you know what time it is?"

He dug an expensive-looking watch out of his vest pocket and popped the cover.

"It's 2:37."

"There'll be enough light to see by in about three-and-a-half hours. Right now, the darkness is our enemy and our friend, but we'll know for sure what we're up against at dawn."

"Do I run now?"

"No," I said, "I need to a minute to figure out the second part of this plan.'"

"Well, for starters, why don't I run out the *back* door?"

I paused and vaguely waved toward the rear of the office, finishing the gesture with my palm up.

"There *isn't* a back door."

His eyes swept all twenty feet of the back wall several times, and then he nodded and said, "*Oh.*"

I was getting a bad feeling about all this, but there was no turning back now.

But while we were inspecting the back of the room I figured out Part Two.

It just might work, I told myself, and if it didn't it would give Carmody a hell of a story to tell at my funeral.

Chapter 54

Out of spite I made Davis take off his pants, too, even though I wouldn't be using them.

I also made him stuff the blanket from the cot through the bars. I wrapped it around me a couple times to add bulk.

There was a quarter moon and it was clear, so there would be enough light to make out shapes. I was tempted to lift one of the slats on the window to gauge the light level, but didn't want to risk drawing fire.

Big cities and some of the bigger towns have coal-gas lamps on the streets, and some places use a couple of outdoor oil lamps burning through the night. In the backwater, though, we relied on the moon, the stars, and light spilling out from whatever building was still illuminated in the late night and early morning.

Right now, that suited me fine.

I pointed my revolver at Judge Gates Davis and motioned for him to come to the front of the cell. He did, stepping on Droopy in the process.

I grabbed him by the hair, not to hurt but to control, and put the gun against his forehead and told him what to do. I told the ones who were conscious and the one I suspected of playing possum that if I heard anything else shouted, anything other than what I wanted, I'd turn and empty my gun into the cell and smear everybody's brains on the bars.

I nodded and Weed blew out the lantern.

We waited a long minute so our eyes could adjust. Then Weed moved to the side of the door before he opened it, or at least I assume that's what he did because that's what I'd told him to do. The office was totally dark, an abyss devoid of any hint of light.

When the door opened, the dim glow from outside actually was a sharp contrast. I could see a wedge of light on the floor.

"Now," I whispered to Davis, making sure he could feel the barrel against his head.

He bellowed.

"Tremaine. I'm coming out first. Don't shoot. He's got a gun in my back."

It was loud and clear. Just for the sake of convenience, so Davis couldn't sabotage my plan, I holstered my gun and punched him in the jaw and he was out before he fell.

The blanket was a dark brown, and I'd draped a corner of it over my head on the theory that in near-darkness it would resemble a mop of long hair. I unearthed my last remaining spare hat, a ratty thing shoved in a file drawer, and shoved it low on my head. The white Daniel Webster sash and white vest under the cutaway coat seemed almost to glow in the faint moonlight coming in the door when I looked down and smoothed them out before I walked out.

Weed, wearing my slightly less ratty hat, which was a few sizes too big and came dangerously close to covering his eyes, was behind me with the rifle.

I told him to walk tall, but he still looked five-six no matter how much he stretched.

And whether I looked like I'd gained fifty pounds by stuffing a blanket under the Daniel Webster getup was to be determined in the next few seconds.

It occurred to me that I might not be able to pull this one off.

Chapter 55

Weed stopped when I did.

My hands were held high. There was a Cooper Pocket revolver stuffed in my left sleeve, my Colt on my hip, another revolver in my waistband, and as much ammunition as I could carry in belts slung around my waist.

Weed broke to his left, and the little fucker wasn't kidding about running like a deer. He was almost to the corner before the men in the shadows could react.

I heard a double pat, the type of sound you'd make by roughly tapping someone on the shoulder. I guessed it was coming from the barber shop across the street, where the door was set back in an alcove. It was all inky black and I could see only the outline of the building and the faint glint from the metal awning.

So I plucked the Cooper out of my sleeve and unloaded all five shots from where I thought the sound had come. While I was firing with my right hand, I pulled the Colt from my waistband with my left and opened up with six more. I kept moving as I fired.

I heard a yelp and a curse, and then quick footsteps.

"This wouldn't have happened if you hadn't run away from him," said a disembodied voice, high and tight and angry and wheezy, and moving to my left.

I fired in the general direction of the voice but shooting by ear at a moving target isn't easy; I'd fired a fusillade when they were sitting still and only managed, from what I could guess, to wing one of them.

And then I heard the thudding of more boots on the boardwalk and thought I saw the outline of that mountain-lion apparition scurry to my left.

I fired a couple more times, just for the hell of it, and ran to my right, toward the Silver Spoon. That's where I needed to go, anyway.

Chapter 56

I reloaded as I ran and pulled out that stupid blanket before it unraveled by itself and tripped me. I'd ditch the cutaway coat as soon as I could because the tail flopped over my holster.

The front doors were locked. The Spoon was equipped with batwings, but like most places that weren't open twenty-four hours a day, the bar had a second set of real doors mounted behind the batwings.

I didn't have a key and didn't have any time to fool around so I kicked in one of the small windows and climbed through it, stepping high so as to avoid a jagged castration.

Elmira wasn't in her room. I went down the hall to her daughter's room. Her daughter, Cassie, didn't live there anymore and the room was now used for clients. I didn't recognize the man in the bed, who mumbled drunkenly and rolled over, but I saw long red hair in the moonlight and recognized it as belonging to a dove named Cecelia.

I shook her awake and she lit a candle.

"Hawke," she said, blinking and scowling, "why are you dressed like Daniel Webster?"

"No time for that. Elmira's not in her room."

"A *course* she ain't in her room," Cecelia said, in a tone that implied she wanted to end the sentence with *stupid.* "She headed out for the Apache camp before closing. Didn't she tell you?"

I turned and left. As I clumped down the stairs I heard some more drunken mumbling and Cecelia say, soothingly, that it was just the dumb marshal.

***

The blacksmith shop was unlocked. I lit a match and found Richard Oak trussed and gagged, lying against the brick hearth.

They'd worked him over pretty good, but he was still alive. I'd left him in charge, and while he was a good man when it came to lifting anvils and the like, this wasn't his type of game.

Tremaine and company had wanted to know what he knew – which was nothing more than I'd left town with, some vague instructions about being in charge – and would have killed him except they planned to come back and try for more later.

I removed the gag. His breathing was deep and regular, but I couldn't bring him to. I decided to cut his ropes and let him rest, but didn't have my knife because one of the goons had liberated it from me while I was unconscious. I lit another match and worked myself into a boil of frustration trying to find something to cut with.

The man had every tool in the world in that shop except something that would cut a rope. Tongs and hammers and picks and shovels and straps and pointy things but *not one fucking knife.*

I lamented that it would take me forever to untie the knots, and if I waited I wouldn't get to…

And then it occurred to me that there was nowhere to go.

Elmira had headed to the Apache camp. In the daytime you could make it in an hour. She was a reasonably competent rider and with the partial moonlight and clear skies I reckoned she could still keep to the trail and make it there in 90 minutes or so. She'd be back with Taza and some cooperative braves by dawn.

Weed was either dead or on the trail to Austin. I had no idea if he was a good rider, but he did manage to make it here on horseback; to hear him talk, if the horse took lame he could run it himself.

Would he really summon Munro and Harbold if he made it? I was betting yes. The man had been duped and was angry and wanted to save his reputation.

It would probably also take him another ninety minutes to get to Austin. I had no idea how long it would take him to find one or both addresses, but he lived there and had nodded when I handed him the paper. It didn't occur to me to ask whether he recognized the streets or was just giving the same reflexive nod he used to acknowledge that he did not see a back door.

But finding an address wasn't such a difficult job. I'd heard there was a new zoo in Austin and I would imagine that if Weed couldn't find a street address he could recruit a gibbon or lemur who could.

If he did manage to locate them, Munro and Harbold would ricochet back here, probably on those magnificent cavalry horses that Munro somehow had extorted from the Army. I figured on a dawn arrival for them, too.

The Canyon Creatures, as Weed called them, were a total wild card. But if Davis had indeed summoned them yesterday afternoon, and if they came, the likely plan of attack would be to use the daylight to travel, camp overnight, and ride in at dawn.

A lot would be happening at dawn, which as far as I could calculate with precision – a task hampered by the fact that one of those assholes stole my watch – would be sometime in the next few hours.

I locked the door to the shop. It was heavy and solid and cumbersome, like everything else in the place, including the owner. I propped Oak up and began to work on the knots.

There was no window, so I wouldn't see the sunlight when it came, but in combat you learn how to take short naps. I decided to get up after a couple hours of sleep and then crack the door open and check.

Chapter 57

The sky was bleeding crimson on the horizon and a few flat clouds were illuminated in the inky sky when I decided to leave.

Oak was conscious but creaky, and badly in need of water, and I planned to get a cup from the rain barrel on the side of the building but I froze and drew my revolver when I heard the footsteps crunching and popping on the strip of gravel that led to the entrance.

"Don't shoot," came Carmody's voice, "I already got so many holes in me I don't need to pee no more. I just leak when I walk."

I was tempted to fling open the door but a suspicion in the reptile vestiges of my mind held me back.

"It's really us," Miller said, "and nobody's got us at gunpoint. Now please open the fucking door."

It took longer than they liked to do that because it's my habit to open doors with an outstretched arm while standing to the side. This door was like something on a bank vault and it was a slow process.

Carmody pushed past me, making sure not to brush the arm that lolled in a sling fashioned from two bandanas. He was followed by Miller, who tugged on the door, gave a double-take, and grunted while he slowly pulled it shut.

"How'd you find me?" I asked.

"Nice to see you, too," Carmody said. "A blind mule walking backwards could have tracked you. Who else would have broken a window at the Spoon and left footprints going in and coming out, and then tracked through wet ground to the door here? It rained maybe twelve or eighteen hours ago but the ground's still damp enough to hold a print. And who would have made tracks with heels that are all worn down on the inside edges, which is a sign of the mighty peculiar way you walk?"

He narrowed his eyes and turned his head sideways a bit.

"And why is you dressed like Daniel Webster?"

Miller interrupted.

"We need to plan. There's about to be a battle bigger than Gettysburg."

I asked him what he was talking about, and he filled me in while Carmody silently slid out the door and came back with water for Oak. He'd appraised what happened without asking and moved quickly. In times when he sees that something needs to be done, Carmody is not one to waste words. He takes care of that process, in a big way, when we're waiting for something to happen and then when the smoke clears.

It was dark in the shop with the door shut but enough harsh light slanted in under the door so Carmody could find a lantern, which I'd been unable to locate the night before.

Miller found some brown wrapping paper on the floor and a pencil on Oak's workbench, right next to, of course, a foot-long knife.

He sketched out the lay of the land in precise circles and arrows and helpfully labelled each party, including "US" in clear block capital letters.

To the west of us were eleven criminal types, he explained, riding in as we spoke.

"They're probably here by now," Miller said, crossing out one circle and drawing a new one.

I told him I got the idea and urged him to continue a little more quickly.

To the east were Munro, Harbold, Weed, and four Apaches.

"And," Miller concluded, tapping the point of the pencil on the greasy brown paper, "this is *us.* "

"Thanks," I said. "You've been busy."

"Carmody doesn't like to waste daylight," Miller explained.

"Do my best sneaking around in those minutes before the sun comes up," Carmody said.

"One other thing," Miller said. "When Carmody was scouting on the road to the west I saw somebody in the center of town. Just standing there, kind of unusual for this time of the morning. I didn't recognize him, and wasn't close enough to see much anyway, but he looked like he was waiting for somebody."

"I'm sure he is," I said, and opened the door to a flood of brilliant sunshine.

Chapter 58

I walked into town while Carmody and Miller rode their extorted horses next to me. I had no idea where my fancy cavalry horse had gone to, other than it had certainly been stolen by now, probably by one of the dopes currently stacked like cordwood in my cell.

I'd taken a drink from the rain barrel and Carmody had given me some jerky, and aside from the dull throbbing where the gun-barrel had been laid across my head I felt pretty good. I'd shed the cutaway coat, vest, and sash, and now had a clean reach to my revolver. I also now stood a chance of being taken seriously.

It looked like I was the catalyst in what was about to follow. I could see riders at one end of Front Street and could see the big Morgans on the other. They began to converge.

When I was new to combat what surprised me most was the businesslike way some confrontations unfolded. I suppose I had expected a frenzied dash to the vortex of battle when combatants first saw each other, and while that sometimes happens it's not the way things usually worked.

Instead, we'd more often than not take up positions in full view of the enemy, sometimes exchanging words and maybe even a pleasantry. On more than one occasion, early in the war, spectators had positioned themselves on the sidelines. Once I saw a man and a woman spread a blanket for a picnic lunch.

And that's how things were unfolding here. I stopped about fifty feet from Tremaine and we circled each other so that I was on Munro's side and Tremaine was grouped among the riders. A couple of them actually sported what looked like sunburns. One, a stocky fellow with a white beard and a mouth that seemed to move constantly, held his left arm cradled in his right, and there was a circle of drying blood on his shoulder.

He let go of his left arm, rested it on the pommel, and with his right hand pointed to Tremaine and then turned his head to talk to the others. I could see the jut of the whiskers that stuck out from his lower lip moving with machine-like regularity. I couldn't make out what he was saying but it was the same creaky, wheezy voice I'd heard in the dark.

Tremaine glared at him.

We were all assembled. As if on cue, Munro pranced his horse forward and one of the outlaws did the same, although his horse did not step as lively and the man's eyes did not mimic Munro's zeal for the pending carnage.

Munro was *smiling*. And then I noticed Lydia. She'd come with him, and seeing as how they both would have had to have awakened in the middle of the night to get here by dawn, I suppose that explained why Munro seemed in such a good mood. A night of revelry with the second-scariest person in the world and the prospect of a bloodbath in the morning were unquestionably his idea of paradise.

Then Tremaine held up a hand and everybody stopped moving, talking, and breathing.

"I've got something to say," Tremaine said. His voice was a powerful baritone and he spoke oddly, given the circumstances, in the formal tones of a stage actor trying to reach the second balcony.

"I've heard some talk amongst some of you, and I know there will be more, so I want to set everybody straight before we commence to settling scores."

He turned toward the dozen or so men sporting sunburns and at least one bullet hole. It was the first time I'd been able to study him close-up. He was younger than I first took him for. The dark walrus mustache put some age on him, but his skin was unlined, and his face still carried some of the firm roundness of youth. His hair was cut short at the sides and his neck was thick and connected with no discernible border to broad, sloping shoulders. I pegged him at not more than thirty.

"Last night, Hawke here hid behind the man that hired me to restore some order here. I ain't blaming Hawke for that. It was a smart move and if

I was about to swap bullets with somebody like me and there was a guy fat as an elephant nearby I'd hide behind him too."

Tremaine shifted his focus to me but still spoke to the balcony.

"I had no choice but to go out the door because Hawke could shoot at me and I couldn't shoot at him, and if there was gunplay, the man I was hired to protect would have been hit."

I could see where this was going.

"At some point," Tremaine said, "Hawke is going to brag that I ran away from him. I hear he likes to get his name in the paper. And I hear he's got a loudmouth deputy who likes to spread stories at the bar."

"Go fuck yourself, asshole," Carmody said.

"And that pencil-neck phony judge switched sides, and I'm sure he's going to be talking big, too."

"Go...go *fuck* yourself," Weed said, tentatively.

Weed straightened up in the saddle and looked around him, gauging the reaction.

"Yes," he piped, "go fuck yourself, *asshole.*"

Tremaine ignored him and squared up toward me. He shook his arms and rolled his shoulders to loosen them up.

"I read that newspaper story about you being 'the man with the lightning draw.' Guess you think you're a pretty big man around here."

"Big war hero, too," Taza said. "But be careful because he kick in knee like little girl."

I decided I would ignore that. For the time being, anyway. First of all, I'd kicked him in the thigh, not the knee. Next time – if there was a next time – I'd aim a few inches higher and plant one where he'd really remember it.

Meanwhile, I figured out why Tremaine was giving a speech. The bastard was embarrassed and wanted to set things right in a one-one-one.

A man can put up with a lot, but for some, embarrassment just eats out their insides. On top of that, Tremaine was a man who made his business from being feared, and damage to his reputation would hurt the wallet as well as the heart.

So now that I knew his motivation, I also knew his weakness and figured I knew how to use it.

He wanted to draw on me.

That was fine, but not yet. I had to up the ante because there was more at stake than just him and me.

So I walked over to him and without breaking stride slapped him across the face.

Chapter 59

There's probably no greater insult to a man than a slap, and Tremaine took it badly.

He was in a bad spot because this wasn't playing out the way he expected. He could, of course, draw on me, as he wanted to do, and I could draw back, but that wouldn't work out for him and his pride: A man hits you with the palm of his hand and you shoot him? That's not very manly.

So he threw a punch. It was a strong punch and was a powerfully built man and the momentum of his blow was spiced with the extra ingredient of blind rage, but the hardest punch in the world doesn't matter if it doesn't land, which it did not. It was a straight right, and was preceded by such a big wind-up that he might as well have mailed me a letter to tell me it was coming.

I stepped inside the punch and it sailed past my ear. Tremaine's momentum carried him forward and I ducked low, pivoted ninety degrees, following the direction of his punch and body, jammed my hip into his groin, and straightened my legs.

A sailor friend I'd sparred with learned that move in Japan and taught it to me. It was from a fighting style they called "gentle way" and it was all about using an opponent's strength and momentum against him.

Tremaine had an excess of both and when I flipped him over my hip I imparted a little altitude by lifting with my legs and my…that man just *flew*.

He landed on his butt, hard. He grunted, and I think he'd had a little wind knocked out of him.

Tremaine didn't really know how to fight. Not this kind of fight, anyway. He should have flipped on his back and regained his breath and composure. He would have been able to kick me with his heels if I'd advanced on him or gone for sidearm if he felt it was necessary.

Instead, he tried to scuttle to his feet with his back to me and of course for a moment he was on all fours with his butt in the air and that's when and where I planted a push-kick.

I'd learned that from someone who'd learned in when he fought it Siam. It's basically the motion you'd use to kick down a door and with a little practice you can generate a lot of power.

I'd practiced a lot.

Tremaine slid forward, flat on his face, at least two feet. The ground was still a little damp and he actually left a furrow.

I backed away, about ten feet.

This time, Tremaine did roll over on his back, looked at me, and I kept my hands away from both guns, the one in my waistband and the one on my hip, as I wagged my fingers upward, motioning for him to get up.

It took him a few seconds, and he wasn't entirely steady. I'm sure that what I did hurt more than his dignity. I do believe I'd heard his tailbone crack when I kicked him.

The guy with the beard and the wheezy voice was laughing. His left hand lay limp on the saddle and he pointed to Tremaine with his right, all the time braying, apparently without the need to breathe. Maybe he was like one of those harmonica players who can make noise blowing or sucking.

He kept laughing for what seemed like a full minute until Tremaine shot him.

Chapter 60

The gun snaked out of Tremaine's holster so fast I could hear it hiss against the leather and I didn't even see the gun level off. It was back in the holster before the sound died away.

Wheezy was still sitting straight up in the saddle and it took a moment for his stiff straight arm to drop.

Despite what you'd expect, head-shot men don't usually get flung backward. Sometimes the impact actually drives them forward, like what happens when you shoot a pail of water off a fencepost. There's a small hole going in but a big one in back where everything gushes out and the bucket will usually fall toward you.

Wheezy had a neat hole between his eyes, so precise it looked like the location had been measured by a craftsman to be perfectly equidistant. After the arm dropped the body followed, as though he were folding up in segments, and when his face hit the mount's crest I noticed that the back of the head was missing.

Chapter 61

I was angry at myself for taking my eyes off Tremaine, although he had immediately holstered his weapon so as to not invite more shooting, at least not at the moment.

The goons were stunned into silence, though some of the horses whinnied and bucked.

The animals had quieted down by the time the body slid off to the ground, one boot still in the stirrup. The horse, uneasy, turned in a circle, dragging it, and then ran away, the body still attached. Nobody made a move to stop it.

Tremaine faced me square again.

I laughed.

Tremaine was shaking, just a little, whether with rage or pain or fear or all three I don't know, but I was happy to see it.

"Who's in charge here?" I asked, apropos of nothing, and the oddity of the question got everyone's attention, including Tremaine's.

"I am," Tremaine said.

He wasn't quite boiling yet, so I wanted to stir the pot a little more.

I looked at what I took to be the oldest man in the gang.

"Is that so?"

I took him by surprise.

"Well, I suppose. I mean, we was taking our orders from…"

He pointed, realized there was nothing there, scanned the near hill, and started to raise his hand toward the running horse and the twisting, bounding body, which had already lost its shirt.

Being dragged by a horse is a demeaning and sickening process. First the clothes get torn off, then the skin.

The older man shrugged.

"Yes, Tremaine's in charge."

I took one small step toward Tremaine. My movement put him on edge, but not enough to pull on me. I knew if I started using my hands again he'd shoot rather than face additional humiliation, but I didn't want to push that far. I just wanted to keep him off balance.

"Tremaine."

I didn't phrase it as a question. I just called it out and made him wonder what comes next.

"Tremaine, you're in charge. How *much* are you in charge?"

He didn't respond.

"Are you willing to raise the stakes? Or are you scared?"

I could see hard knotty muscles in his jaw pulsing.

"What the fuck are you talking about?"

"Tremaine, we have twenty men on this street and if we start a running gun battle everyone could die – plus who knows how many bystanders killed by stray shots. And if these assholes win who knows what they'll do to the innocent people in town. I know that means nothing to you, but these are my friends and my…"

It was then that I noticed Elmira standing under an awning and I took a minute to search for the word.

"My friends and my loved ones."

Tremaine turned his head and spit.

"So?"

"So I want two things: Gillis and Davis. I want Davis to go to jail for attempted murder and theft of government property, and I want Gillis so I can beat the shit out of him."

"So?" Tremaine spat again. "What's this to me?"

"*You* want Davis and the counterfeit money he stole. Not because you want the money. You probably couldn't spend it or wouldn't want to take the risk. It's because that's the one piece of evidence that incontrovertibly ties your boss into a criminal enterprise. Not that you can about that, either, but you've been hired to fix this for him."

"I'm running out of patience," Tremaine said. "Get to the point."

"If you're man enough, let's just make this you and me, right now where we stand. If you kill me, you can have Davis. You can have Gillis, too, if you want him. The key to the cell is in my pocket."

"What about the money?"

"My deputy will show you. I don't know where it is myself."

Tremaine snorted a mirthless laugh.

"Sure he will."

"I'm way ahead of both of you," Carmody said, riding up beside us and opening a dirt-encrusted oilskin bag. "I seen where this was going and took the liberty of fetching it just now so Marshal Hawke can get to the business of blowing your head off.'"

I hadn't realized Carmody had been gone.

Carmody reached into the bag and fanned some of the money so Tremaine could see it.

"Not more than fifty feet away. Buried in in back of the outhouse. Nobody ever wanders back there, believe you me."

"Suppose after I kill you your friends go back on the deal," Tremaine asked.

"I could ask you the same question," Harbold said.

I spread my hands.

"Then we're no worse off than before we made the deal. Then we all go back to war and kill each other."

"You've got nothing to lose," I said to the goons, "and everything to gain. I don't know how many of you are from the canyon, but I see a few of you with charred pant-legs, so you've got an idea what the people fighting on my side are capable of."

Horses can sense emotions, and a few of the outlaws' mounts began shifting and taking small, agitated steps.

"Maybe we should listen to him, Mr. Tremaine," one of the men said.

I pointed to Taza.

"And if you think these combat veterans are tough, wait until my Apache friends get through with you."

Taza smiled broadly.

"Tremaine and Hawke shoot it out … sounds like a good idea," another outlaw said.

"And we've got one more to even up the numbers. Lydia Davis, the woman you kidnapped, is here, and she's got a gun and a grudge."

"Lots of guns," she said, riding to the front of the pack. She held a Sharps rifle aloft, pointed to a Colt .45 on her hip, and displayed an impressive scowl.

There was some mumbled conversation among the outlaws. I heard the words *hell, yes* spoken a few times.

And then the pack divided and they moved to each side of the street, out of the expected line of fire.

"I was looking forward to this," Munro said, pulling on the reins, and moving alongside where I stood. "You wrecked all the fun."

And then he whispered low so only I could hear, leaning down as I walked back a few paces to the spot where I'd stand.

"Guess this isn't our first battle by proxy. You're doing the right thing. There are people like us and then there are the regular people – pastors, schoolteachers, women, children. We fight so they don't have to. And now you're fighting so *we* don't have to, which normally would piss me off but this time you're right. This entire shithole town of yours would be killed in the crossfire, right down to the last dog and cat."

"Thanks for the pep talk," I said. "I get the feeling you're going to rub some liniment on my shoulders and remind me to not to drop my left hand when I throw my right."

"Something like that," Munro said. "All I can tell you is that he's a show-off. He's in a quiet, white-hot rage, and now he not only wants you dead, but he wants it to be spectacular. He wants to make the papers. Like you did."

Munro guided his horse over to the board-walk, and as he pulled away he said, *"Work on his head."*

I looked at Tremaine and stepped back until we were sixty feet apart. In my business you get to gauge distances pretty well, and it may have been fifty-nine or sixty-one but not more either way, and it was the distance at which I'd done most of my practice.

Tremaine didn't move. Maybe he liked the distance, too, or just didn't think about such things, but it occurred to me after seeing him shoot that bearded mouth-runner that I was going to need every advantage I could get.

"I'm giving you a chance to back out, Tremaine," I said. "You're a dead shot against somebody who's sitting on a horse and not even looking at you, but I'm not one of the cooperative victims your kind feeds on."

He almost went for his gun at that point; I sensed as much as saw it.

Contrary to what you read in dime novels there's no real etiquette in a shootout. The good guy doesn't have to wait for the bad guy to pull first. And it's not so much about who pulls first but rather who lands first, and who lands where it counts and often how many times you land where it counts.

Pulling on me while we were jawing, though, might be interpreted by some as jumping the gun with a cheap shot, and reputation was what was on the line for him right now. I think his life was secondary to him at that instant.

I figured the longer I kept talking, the madder he'd get and the better chance I'd have of getting out of this unperforated.

"You've got nothing to be ashamed of, Tremaine. The price of hubris is destruction. Just walk away."

Tremaine said nothing, but I had a feeling he didn't follow.

"It means 'excessive pride,' you dumb shit," Carmody said.

"Shut up and shoot," Tremaine said.

"Try only to make big wound and not kill him," Taza shouted. "So I can torture him later."

The outlaws laughed, and Munro guffawed in his thundering bass.

With my left index finger, I pointed to a spot between my eyes, then pointed at Tremaine, and made the universal shooting gesture with my empty hand.

"I'm going to give you a third eye, Kid, and there's not a damn thing you can do about it."

I hadn't finished when Tremaine lost the battle with his demons of rage and drew.

Chapter 62

As I've said, timing is everything.

I wasn't that much concerned about who drew first because I pretty much knew that I couldn't physically out-shoot him. But this wasn't a quick-draw contest or target match.

He gave it away when he leaned forward just a bit. Some shooters do that unconsciously to bring the right leg back a bit, allowing a little more room for the barrel to clear the holster.

As soon as I saw the tell-tale I dropped to one knee, pulling as I did so.

I banked on the fact that he'd want to finish me with one spectacular headshot, especially as I'd goaded him into believing that I'd try the same.

As I've undoubtedly said before, coincidences do happen, which is presumably why we invented the word.

For the third time in as many weeks, some son of a bitch had shot my hat off.

Chapter 63

I fired and rolled and came up on a knee again, this time with the gun from my waistband in my left hand.

Tremaine hadn't expected either the drop or the roll.

Nor did he expect the bullet that caught him in the thigh.

I knew he'd go for my head, trying to end the confrontation with a shot he could gloat over and recount in bar-rooms for years to come.

And I'm sure his bullet would have burrowed right between my eyes had I not moved before I tried to get off a shot.

I hit him again in the stomach and fired with both hands.

But my left hand wasn't working. And then I felt the pain.

It works that way sometimes, especially in the heat of battle. Whatever part of the mind that insulates one's sanity delays the pain long enough for you deal with the fact that you're in trouble.

I shot again with my right hand, barely keeping my balance, and missed.

Tremaine showed no emotion as he stumbled, fought to keep his balance, and raised his revolver.

A man can get off a lot of shots in the time it takes to die, and he sent off two that snaked into the ground about ten feet in front of me. Sometimes they skid and bounce back up, and they would have caught me where it hurt with me hunkered down like that, but they just buried themselves.

I emptied my revolver and believed I saw him start to fall. I picked up the gun I'd dropped and emptied that into him, too, and the last thing I remembered was clicking five, six, maybe ten times on expended chambers. I believe I was still pulling the trigger when I fell forward.

That's what they told me later, anyway.

Chapter 64

It had been a clean through-and-through shot and I could move around all right in a couple days.

Carmody said that I had been envious of the attention he'd received and accused me of somehow contriving to get wounded too.

Actually, I'd been hit higher and the round had broken my collarbone but not torn too much muscle, so my movement wasn't impaired much. Carmody's wound had ripped through his arm and chest muscle and he would likely have trouble reaching forward for some time, but he'd eventually heal up, according to the doctor who'd treated him in Gray Springs, who I tended to believe.

Carmody had been treated by a doctor who had an office and a haircut and a diploma on the wall. My physician was an itinerant who rode by every week or so. He was a disheveled little man whose hair hung in his eyes and also, I am told, treated cattle as well as people and was vague about his qualifications for either job.

In any event, I could do pretty much anything I wanted as long as I could tolerate the white-hot pain that went along with the process.

I had a little trouble with the bass parts played with my left hand but could still passably navigate the upright piano in the Spoon. Most of the time I'd play cowboy tunes or folk ditties we'd sung during the war but there's only so much material in that vein so when I ran dry I'd throw in some Beethoven or Mozart. If you keep a nice steady beat and play loudly enough – a process Carmody called cowpoking it up – even Chopin sounds like perfectly acceptable dance-hall music.

But tonight, Carmody informed me that I was not up to par. He leaned on the piano and spoke to me ital sotto voce.

"Can't you pound out a pick-me-up tune? Take a look around. This stuff is making people want to slit their wrists. Maybe slit yours too, while they're at it, so I'd be careful."

"It's German music," I said. "They are a very melancholy people."

"I know it's German. It's Wagner, and it makes me want to just set the place on fire and die tragic and all while I yowl like a coyote."

"How the hell do you know this stuff?"

"I ain't no dummy. I look rough, but I've been to a few concerts, I read some, and I see things. Right now I see there's something eating you."

"No," I lied, "not really."

"Suppose the shoulder don't make your mood no better. I know this is kind of obvious, but if you have to grit your teeth when you play maybe you could back off them ivories for a few weeks."

"An artist must suffer for his work," I said, and Carmody shrugged and walked away.

I decided to heighten the gloom with some Tchaikovsky and after a few more trail-hands finished their beers and walked out Elmira apparently figured she had no choice but to intervene.

We'd spoken very little in the past few days, only perfunctory stuff, and events had recently conspired to further darken my mood.

She sat next to me on the bench and looked straight ahead.

At least she didn't try to sing. She is tone-deaf and can't recognize it, which is part of being tone-deaf, and makes wild-animal sounds when she attempts to harmonize. I was pounding out a death scene from an opera, though, and maybe her style would have fit it.

"I've told you that I'm sorry," she said.

"Yes, you have."

I played a little louder.

"I've told you that Gillis lied, he said everything would be for our own good in the long run. And it *sounded* good. I believed that he was just trying to establish some order in town and straighten out this railroad mess. I believed him."

"You fell for him. You swallowed all that stuff about how much he cared for women when you knew he slapped the girls around when he got drunk. You believed all that crap about him wanting to help the town when you knew he was in it for himself."

She sensed this was going nowhere, following the same path as the last half-dozen or so conversations we'd had on the matter, and before she started talking about big pictures and greater truths, she gave up and changed topics.

"Look," she said, "let's just enjoy tonight. Your friends should be here soon."

"I imagine you're looking forward to that more than I am."

She didn't get my meaning, and as subtlety is largely wasted on her I dispensed with it.

"You've been spending a lot of time with Tom lately."

"Carmody? My God, Josiah, I like him but you're –"

"*Harbold*. Tom Harbold. I heard one of the girls say you were out with him all morning yesterday. Having a picnic or something."

She laughed. For real.

"Josiah, I didn't even know 'Tom' is Harbold's first name. And yes, we were out all morning. I'll show you why."

She returned in a minute with my Boss of the Plains hat and laid it atop the piano.

"Carmody, who I am not sneaking around with either, told me how upset you were that you lost your hat when you were ambushed. Carmody can't really ride much until he heals up, so he told Constable Harbold about where the ambush happened. We went out to look for it together. I found it stuck on a tree branch."

I stopped playing, thanked her and put it on.

Then I kissed her.

It was a great hat, especially in the heat. There's a sweatband on the inside and the crown is very high, which allows for air to move around to keep your head cool.

And the bullet hole would probably help with ventilation, too.

Chapter 65

Weed, Harbold, Carmody, Munro, and Lydia Davis pulled a table and chairs over to the piano so we could talk while I played. Elmira said she would be over in a minute.

The bargirl stopped at Weed first. He was undecided and took a moment to look around.

"I'll have a mug of whiskey," he said.

Carmody cleared his throat.

"Whiskey in places like this is a little tough to guzzle by the mug. Maybe a mug of cold beer would be a mite more refreshing. Been a hot day."

"All right," Weed said. "I usually don't tell people this, but I don't have a lot of experience in these kinds of places."

"We'll keep that to ourselves," Carmody said.

Weed loosened up a little after a few drinks. We all did.

Munro filled us in on what was happening in Austin. Gates Davis was in jail. Harbold had arrested him personally.

"Good," said Lydia, who actually *was* drinking whiskey by the mug. "He's an asshole."

Jefferson Gillis was in jail, too. Harbold couldn't figure out any charges that would stick and was anxious to let Gillis go so he could watch me beat the shit out of him, but it turned out there were four warrants out for him on various fraud charges in Texas and New Mexico.

And on the subject of beatings, I satisfied Munro's curiosity about Taza. In return for his help with the ersatz cannons, I agreed to teach him what I knew of Siam kickboxing so he could practice for the storied day on which he would beat me to death.

Munro had some good news: There was a thousand-dollar reward for the capture of Tremaine, dead or alive, and as I'd arranged the former circumstance, Munro told me, it would be coming my way.

But he tempered it with some bad news. The railroad project was delayed, held up in byzantine politics. While it was still likely that it would pass through Elmira's property, turning her scrub back lot into a bonanza, it was no longer a certainty.

Powerful political forces from other constituencies wanted a piece of the pie, he said, and were lobbying to re-draw the map to benefit their districts.

Elmira wasn't disturbed about the money, she said, and it was the truth. She had a comfortable business and could pay the bills and never worried about such things much, anyway.

But then her expression changed as a thought struck her, and she betrayed an infinite sadness.

"That means that all this killing was for *nothing*," she said.

"It usually is," Munro said, and the indisputable authority of his words, spoken with a voice that had commanded hundreds of men to march and ride to their deaths, hung in the air like the resonant peal of a bell.

He looked at the table while he talked, an odd posture for a man who usually made militant eye contact, drilling those blue orbs right into you.

"Last year they tried to kill Hawke because there was money to be made and he was in the way. I understand that. I don't approve of it, but I understand it."

"But this time," Elmira said, her thought trailing off.

"This time it was for revenge. And something else. Hawke had a good word for it: 'hubris.'"

Carmody, who I thought had been asleep, raised a finger.

"It means…"

"I know what it means," Munro snapped, and Carmody went back to sleep.

Munro looked at Elmira.

"It's what I see all the time at the statehouse, the same shit that I saw at that canyon, and exactly what I saw happen down the street here a few days ago. Battles we get caught up in even though they're not our battles, and we might not even remember how they started, for Christ's sake. We just sit and fight blindly. In the long shadows of greed and revenge."

Lydia took another pull of whiskey from her mug.

"This is getting pretty fucking depressing," she said, wiping her mouth with the back of her hand and looking over at me.

"Can't you play something else besides this fucking *funeral* music?"

I cowpoked up some Chopin, the Military Polonaise, a sort of march that's set to the beat of a cheerful Polish dance. It's long and loud and if you play it broadly it sounds like it was written for a saloon on Saturday night.

"I like that better," Elmira said, and I saw her let out a breath. "It's over, and we've got a lot to be thankful for. We all got through it alive…"

"My asshole father's in jail," Lydia said.

"That too," Elmira agreed, and when I looked closer, I realized that in the past hour or so she had not only become cheerful but blind drunk.

"And I'm grateful for to have all you wonderful, honest people around me, even if you do seem to enjoy shooting people more than is normal."

Weed was on his fourth beer and was almost as unfocused as Elmira.

"I second that," he said, and then turned serious.

"And I apologize for what I did. I was under Davis's spell, I guess. I believed him when he told me that everything was all legal. I honestly didn't know that the money from Gillis was a bribe. Davis told me that's how frontier judges got paid, and of course I was excited to move onto something bigger than settling property and mineral rights claims. I thought I was doing the right thing."

"I know," Elmira said, the words coming a little thickly as happens when she drinks too much and her lips fall asleep.

"I believed somebody too, because I thought what he said sounded good, even though what he did and said were two different things."

She shook her head.

"It was a bad experience," she said.

***

When you're in combat, it takes all the strength you have to go counter to what you really want to do, which in most cases is running away from, and not toward, people who are trying to kill you. The mark of a good soldier is the ability to overcome your natural instincts.

And so I mustered every ounce of resolve I possessed and was able to overcome the temptation to tell her it was for her own good.

Instead, I cowpoked up some cheerful Mozart.

I was suddenly in a very good mood.

THE END

About the Author

Carl Dane is a career journalist and author who has written more than 20 nonfiction books, hundreds of articles, and a produced play. He's worked as a television anchor and talk show host, newspaper columnist, and journalism professor.

He was born in San Antonio, Texas, and has maintained a lifelong interest in the Old West and the Civil War. He is a member of The Sons of Union Veterans and has traced many of ancestors not only to the Civil War, but also to the War of 1812 and the American Revolution.

Carl often writes and lectures about ethical dilemmas, and has a deep interest in morality, including questions of whether the ends justify the means and how far a reasonable person can go in committing an ostensibly wrong act to achieve a "greater good."

He has testified on ethical issues before the U.S. Congress and has appeared on a wide variety of television programs, including Fox News' *The O'Reilly Factor*, *ABC News World News Now*, *CBS Capitol Voices*, and CNN's *Outlook*.

Carl is also interested in the structure of effective and eloquent communication, and has written two recent books on professional writing and speaking for a commercial academic and reference publisher.

Reviewers have consistently praised his work for its deft humor.

When not coyly writing about himself in the third person, Carl lives in suburban New Jersey, where he is active in local government and volunteer organizations. He is the father of two sons.

The characters of Josiah Hawke and Tom Carmody – and the situations they confront – were drawn from the author's interest in the darker sides of the human soul, and the contradictions built into the psyche of every man and woman.

Hawke is an intellectual, a former professor of philosophy, who became drawn to the thrill of violence after the life-changing events of the Civil War – which not only exposed Hawke to violence but showed him that he possessed considerable untapped skill in that area. Carmody, yin to Hawke's yang, is a blunt backwoodsman who is no stranger to violence, either, but has fought for survival and not for sport. Carmody wonders if Hawke's philosophical justifications are merely a smokescreen for seeking out trouble – and he's not afraid to tell that to Hawke.

Follow Carl at www.carldane.com

Made in the USA
Columbia, SC
24 December 2018